DOSTOEVSKY'S LAST NIGHT

D1310981

DOSTOEVSKY'S LAST NIGHT

CRISTINA PERI ROSSI

Translated by Laura C. Dail

PICADOR USA
New York

DOSTOEVSKY'S LAST NIGHT. Copyright © 1992 by Cristina Peri
Rossi. Translation © 1994 by Laura C. Dail. All rights reserved.
Printed in the United States of America. No part of this book may
be used or reproduced in any manner whatsoever without written
permission except in the case of brief quotations embodied in
critical articles or reviews. For information, address Picador USA,
175 Fifth Avenue, New York, N.Y. 10010.

Picador® is a U.S. registered trademark and is used by St. Martin's
Press under license from Pan Books Limited.

ISBN 0-312-14322-2

First published by Grijalbo Mondadori in 1992

First Picador USA Paperback Edition: July 1996

10   9   8   7   6   5   4   3   2   1

Gambling is the first experience of freedom in the physical world.

—DOSTOEVSKY
Notes From the Underground

DOSTOEVSKY'S LAST NIGHT

That night the bingo hall was packed. I detest weekends; that's when the middle-class families come in droves, the good, plain folks, who set their hearts on winning a round of bingo with a few measly dollars. But don't think for a second these are the *real* gamblers; they are simply weekend dilettantes. They could just as well go to the movies, visit a sick relative or see a musical. They barge into the casino in clusters, like mini-brigades. Usually they come in groups of four: the obese husband, the portly wife, their newlywed sons or daughters, who already betray a sense of tedium, vaguely resentful of frustration inflicted by their own cowardice or lack of imagination. Upon entering the gaudy red room, wading through the glaring lights, the founding couple puffs up with the mediocre satisfaction at having brought up a couple of kids, for having set them on the respectable path of marriage and a career. This game of bingo emerges as nothing more than one of those little pardonable sins, a little bourgeois fun, perhaps the closest they ever come to danger and passion. It's like taking the whole family to a whorehouse. They're noisy and obnoxious. They strut around smugly with the obscure advantage of never having strayed off society's precious path. They are nothing like the true gambler: the loner who hates company or crowds of any kind, who reserves all his concentration for his encounters with luck.

When these middle-class squadrons and their offspring invade the room, I do not like to play. If I happen to find a table free, one of those with the plush green runners, I sit there alone and erect a kind of fortress around the boards (I play with three, four or an entire series, depending on the occasion), to protect myself from these intruders. As obvious as possible, I place the big aluminum ashtray on one side, the black lacquer cup of red and green markers on the other, and tear sheets of paper from the house notepads and line them up to form a kind of makeshift fence around my boards. But to no avail. Inevitably, one of these annoying, raucous families finds its way to the empty seats at my table. On weekends the place is bursting at the seams. Without fail, when people get together in groups, whether bonded by family, shared political views, or just because they root for the same team, they become presumptuous, triumphant, domineering. Of course I can't refuse to let them sit down at my table; bingo's a democratic game, after all. But from that moment on, I lose my appetite for playing. Any combat with one's luck requires absolute concentration: it is a solitary duel with no place for emotions, pity, or even sex. For these middle-class families, however, gambling is like an orgy; a pastime they can all share together—incestuously. Infatuated with themselves, they holler silly family anecdotes at each other, laugh, belch, and carry on. But underneath it all lingers an obscene kind of lust, one that simmers just beneath the surface of familial propriety. For them, to share a gambling table sanctioned by the State is like committing the dark, original sin that they hide, in the name of law and order. Just look at the way they share their bingo boards. A real gambler would never share a board. Sensitive to luck's obscure maneuvers, he knows that bingo boards and playing cards contain a sacred code granted by the gods, a unique and individual gift. These weekend bingoers haven't a clue about that. The father who harbors secret desires for his daughter spreads out two boards for her on the green table with his sweaty hands, his eyes flashing. And all the while, the younger fellow, the girl's hubby, lowers his head in humiliation, deferring to the old man's seniority and privilege as a father. And then there's the perverse old cow, the wicked mother, who flirts with her dear son-in-law about numbers, not bothering to blush at the obscene connotations of some of them. And finally the young couple, each clutching their respective boards, reveal their rivalry and selfishness with impunity.

On weekends I just have to be patient and wait until the room empties of these casual betters. Usually, around twelve o'clock, the families clear out. They don't like to stay out too late. They leave the way they came—in bunches. They gather their coats, make snide remarks about gambling (they're sore losers), and slip back into their repressed, habitual roles. They've already forgotten those few illicit hours of merrymaking; when the old lady finally blossomed into what she had always dreamt of being—a mancharmer, manipulating them with her firm, erect breasts; when the old, docile ox could play at being Jupiter in love with his own daughters. Even the son-in-law in those enchanted hours could cease being the sniveling, pale functionary he was, and the daughter, domesticated by marriage, could let her slimy, complacent father drool over her and caress her cheeks.

Once gone, only the true men and women gamblers are left. A great sigh of relief echoes through the hall. True gambling men and true gambling women do not need company; all they need is solitude and concentration, entangled as they are in the frenetic battle with chance. Sex has no place here. Each player wants a table to himself, a solitary stakeout. He accepts no other companionship than the ashtray, a cigarette, his lighter, and a pen to jot down the magical, rebellious numbers. Apart from these, only an occasional glass of whiskey, a beer, or ice water will do. Dueling with fate makes one thirsty.

His eyes remain fixed on the television screen where the sumptuous numbered balls rhythmically appear, one by one. He has ears for nothing but the monotonous voice of the speaker, who, like some rigorously professional stewardess, intones the numbers in one sustained note, betraying not the slightest emotion. Every player, tense and feverish, funnels his emotion into that table where the numbers appear in succession, in some mysterious order of chance, in some combination of luck which we do not know, which we do not intuit, and which is an indecipherable mystery.

At two in the morning nobody's left but us die-hard gamblers, the avowed, the fanatics, the mystics. "Temples of Chance" is what they call casinos from Monte Carlo to Saigon. We true gamblers are a tight-lipped, solitary bunch. We would never make glib remarks about luck; on the contrary, we stand arrogant and proud before her. When we lose, we do so with dignity; no insults, no curses. We don't

4

lash out at number six because it didn't show up, or rail against number twenty-nine when it refused to leave the screen. Likewise, when the true gambler wins, he doesn't brag or carry on or make a spectacle of himself. He knows that winning and losing are simple facts beyond commentary. In any case, winning or losing conforms to a metaphysical law against which human judgment is helpless. It's not about justice or work or efficiency or method. It's *something else*. That something else can't be categorized; there are no symbols to express it. Only apparent indifference suits this order of luck; one must remain undaunted by losing, undaunted by winning. Chance mirrors the disorder of the world: one person happens to be born into a rich family, another is born destitute. One person gets cancer, another has a gift for science. There are theories that profess to have an explanation for such mysteries: religion, history, biology. But in spite of those theories, life remains irreducible—a veritable chaos. The guy whose bingo board wins the prize doesn't know any more about these mysteries than the guy who loses. Winning or losing are not revelations: there is no accessible truth about luck. Nor is there in other disciplines. The Christian or Buddhist, the doctor or bureaucrat, the soldier or politician, man or woman doesn't know any more about the mystery of existence than anybody else, as the worm has no clue about how he produces silk, or the elephant about how he makes ivory.

The fact that luck is irreducible provokes in most gamblers an irrepressible tendency toward fetishism and superstition. For example, I know a roulette player who is convinced that he can win only when he's wearing the black necktie his grandmother from Kansas gave him. If he should lose while wearing it, he doesn't attribute his bad fortune to the long, delicate fetish. However, when luck works in his favor, he swears that it is all due to the hidden powers of that fine little tie.

Many gamblers carry amulets in their pockets: their mother's wedding ring, their wife's lighter, a sandalwood fan, striped socks. They feel a predilection for a particular table, a special pen, or a certain piece of clothing. (Tai Hing, the famous opium smoker and Chinese boss of the casinos in Macao, was convinced that the color red brought luck to the gamblers, while green and white favored the gambling house. He forbade the use of red in any of his casinos or advertisements.)

I myself am subject to these superstitions. This magical thinking overcomes us whenever we're feeling insecure or grasp how puny we are before the disproportionately great forces of fate. "The brunette selling the bingo boards brings me luck" or "Table twenty-three is charmed" are manifestations of this irrational thinking. (But the same happens when we come down with a serious illness; the fat priestess will cure us with a laying-on of hands, or that herb paste from India will do the trick, or that miracle water preciously stored away in a little unmarked flask.)

One spell, during which I lost almost every night, I attributed to a honey-colored tweed jacket that until then, at least, had been a very comfortable jacket and fit me quite well. I began to eye it suspiciously when number twenty-two didn't appear and so blamed all my bad luck on that jacket. Finally, I tossed it to the back of the closet and exchanged it for another. Of course, these subtle relationships can't be proven scientifically; the order of chance is irrational and mysterious, like faith. The gambler counts only his successes, never his failures, the same as healers or fortune-tellers or politicians.

So it seems that some of the ladies who sell the boards are more auspicious than others. If one smiles at us or makes some flattering remark, we think she *knows* that we're going to hit the jackpot that night. If she gives us the brush-off or looks away, it's a sure sign that she's picked somebody else to be the recipient of her fortune. The tendency to employ women in gambling halls has virtually religious symbolism. For the professional gambler, the casino or the bingo hall is a temple where his passion to win and to decipher destiny is a substitute for prayer. Like temples, gambling halls are replete with sensual stimulants. The intricate chandeliers glitter like votive candles, cigarette smoke wafts upward like clouds of incense from censers, the plush crimson carpets and chairs swallow one up and muffle all sound except for the priestly voice chanting like a litany, reciting the sacred numbers of the balls. In pagan temples, the vestal virgins guarded the secrets of destiny. In gambling halls, the board sellers are the minor deities of the temple; they remain unruffled in their arbitrary dispensation of grace, never flinching. They treat all customers with generic equanimity, maintaining a stolid distance so that no one feels specially protected. With supreme imperturbability, they put up with the nervous players who try to seduce them and win their favors by touching their hands or caressing their arms. Since these minor goddesses are pledged to act with indifference, the addicts try to decode minute details and subconscious gestures that might reveal some sign of the benevolence of fortune or the punishment of loss.

I myself am often prone to these kinds of interpretations. For example, just the other night, after losing for two hours straight, I decided to have a glass of water and pop an aspirin I'd been carrying in my pocket. At that very moment, the board seller at my table, the virginal brunette with those intense black eyes, smiled at me and said compassionately: "I have a headache too." While I was buying boards for the next round, I offered her an aspirin with a slight motion of the hand. I couldn't detain her; she has to be very quick on her feet, but later, when the numbers were slowly, mechanically, being called out, like the counting of a rosary, she slipped over to my table and took an aspirin from the little case. It seemed a good omen. I felt that from then on I had a much better chance of winning. If she had chosen me for the aspirin, surely she would return the favor by offering me the prize. On the next round, a person at the adjoining table won. She cast me a look full of pity—I thought I saw it in her eyes. The calculation was off by a difference of one board. Her intentions were good, but the winning board was given to somebody else right next to me. In any case I thanked her, mentally. From that point on, I knew I wouldn't win that night. Luck had only grazed me. Her soft breath, her caresses never visit a player twice.

"There is a moment, a single instant when fortune smiles on us. It's a question of knowing exactly when to seize the opportunity and when to pull out," says Carlos, a cool and efficient gambler.

I don't talk much about gambling with Carlos, in spite of our mutual addiction. As gamblers we couldn't be more different, like two parishioners who attend the same church. They are alike only in space and time, but they make love differently, approach God differently, even their way of suffering or enjoying religious ceremonies is totally different. Carlos is a vain gambler. He scorns luck. He only plays because he's bored. He's not into discovering mysterious secrets in the distribution of luck, nor does he look for hidden symbols in the act of gambling. No, he's just fleeing a monotonous and insufferable tedium that he attributes to the world, to his profession (he's a dentist), to conventional marriage and to his sedentary life. But in reality this only reflects a cold, unresponsive soul. He plays with disdain and aloofness, the same way he peers into a mouth full of cavities or examines an X-ray of a dislocated jaw. He avoids staining his white bib with the blood or pus from his patients the same way he avoids falling in love or losing what he's just won gambling. He has an inexorable faith in himself, in his superiority over fate; that's why he wins so often. He's vain, but not proud. When he wins he doesn't return for several days. If I win, on the other hand, I'm intoxicated and try to repeat the performance. My ambition is boundless; it's not about winning once but always. Winning one prize means nothing to me. I want every prize, every success.

"I simply try to win sometimes and lose other times, the way it usually works out anyway," Carlos says. "But you, what you're after, what you want, is impossible to tell."

What I'm looking for, Carlos, is very easy to say—to win over and over again, to break the bank, to destroy the normal mechanics of facts. You only want to kill your boredom; I want to kill God.

Every once in a while, Carlos tries to hook up with one of the casino employees. In his eyes any one of them will do. He's not very demanding when it comes to romance, just as he doesn't demand much from luck. He never talks about these fleeting, passionless affairs. I, on the other hand, am an ascetic; never an insinuation or equivocal gesture. These little goddesses, these dispensers of luck or misfortune are, for me, only instruments of a much greater, more absolute power. The passion for the game keeps me so enthralled that there's no room for other passions. When I win, I put my bid on the silver tray the dealer passes to me, and when

9

I lose, I retire in silence after one last game, without revealing my bad mood. A closer, more intimate relationship with these divine beings, these guardians of fortune, would make me uncomfortable. Consorting with them would be like superimposing levels, eliminating the highest. You don't traffick in the illusory unless you want to kill it.

"Sometimes," I say to Carlos in one of those rare moments when we're having a few drinks in the casino bar, "at the gambling table I feel like I'm on an airplane with stewardesses running around like protective mothers consoling the passengers when they get airsick, explaining the air route to them, or dispensing tranquilizers to the anxious."

I believe I've detected certain disdainful looks given by some of the board sellers, as if we players occupying the leather seats were patients in an oncology ward or incurable guests at an insane asylum. It's only a fleeting glance though. Perhaps at times they do despise us: autistic, crazy children fanatically dependent on those balls that arbitrarily spin out of that electronic cylinder. But, like love, contempt and admiration have little to do with the object, and reveals more about the person feeling it than about the object itself. The same thing happens to me. There are days when I detest gambling. I don't want to be anywhere near a gambling house. Sometimes I find this addiction infantile and ridiculous. There are other days, however, when I wake up feeling a terrible anxiety and can't wait for time when I can be alone with a slot machine (as if it were a lover), when I can caress it, seduce it, listen to it sing, plug it with coins like bullets, strip it, humiliate it, rape it. Those nights when I leave work exhausted and dizzy, and the brilliant lights of the bingo parlor flood over me like the bewitching lights of a brothel, I immerse myself in them and even pay for a pleasure I don't always obtain. I brandish the red pen—a penis on fire—and I listen, attentive, to the infernal succession of the numbers. Four. Twenty-eight. Sixty-nine. Sixteen. Fifty-four. "Bingo!" A murmur fills the room like the cooing of pigeons in heat. I plunge my hand into my pocket. I've only got ten dollars left. But I have my credit card. There is always a bank with twenty-four-hour service near casinos. We inveterate losers resort to them like the chronically ill to emergency rooms. I leave the hall. It's freezing outside. Dazzled by the harsh lights and the video screens of the casino, once outside, I feel like a ghost on a street in a strange city. Automatically, I head for the nearest bank. I open the door with my ID card. I run to the cash machine. I enter my secret number. (I've chosen an easy one, the year I was born, to save time in circumstances such as these.) I can't stand the short wait for the machine to spit out the cash. Once I've stuffed the money in my pocket, I breeze back to the casino, like an exhale. Luckily, the entrance is still open (which means the next game hasn't begun yet).

Gamblers are fanatics; we can't lose time, we can't sit out a single game. We're afraid that the lapse during our absence could well have been fortune's chosen moment to favor us, the game we would have won. The guy who quits before the place shuts down or before he's lost everything is not a real gambler. For him gambling's just a hobby. I left my coat on the chair (at table number twenty-three, my favorite) so that nobody would steal my place. I return to the casino and run directly to my table. I don't have time for—nor do you win by—looking around at the other players. I look anxiously at the board seller and before sitting down I gesture to her to leave four boards on the table. I've lost too much money tonight; I've got to try to recoup it. I'm not trying to win anymore, just not to lose. The board sellers swoop like pigeons over asphalt cooing, "Last board, last board." The nervous players raise their hands to buy a board to tempt luck with one they didn't get in the distribution. The superstitious gambler is one of two kinds: either he's one of those who always buys the last board hoping that maybe this time it will be the lucky one, or he's one who never buys the last board because the word "last" sounds too ominous. (I belong to both classes: one minute I think the last board is going to win, the next minute it is doomed.)

While they start to announce the numbers from the central table, I calculate how much money I've already lost. If I get bingo, I will have won it back. But I might not win and the night will end in disaster. I promise myself from this moment on I will be a moderate gambler. I will leave my credit cards at home so I only bet the exact amount I have pre-planned. But if what has happened before happens again, luck will approach me the instant I'm without a single cent, and I'll have missed the opportunity when it would have brushed up against me with her cloak, her breath, her hips, her neck, her breasts, her hair. In all mythologies, fortune is a woman. In all mythologies, one has to seduce her. Nervous, apprehensive, restless, we besiege her with our phallus erect, our mouth drooling, our promises: "If you favor me," we promise, not believing ourselves, "I'll never play again. I will be a prudent, hard-working, viceless man. I'll go to bed early, save money, quit smoking, visit the family."

Luck is a woman, and in order to win her favor just once, like desperate, longing lovers, we invoke her with promises, with vows, with incantations. But she doesn't believe us. She's a woman and she doesn't believe us. Why should she? She knows perfectly well that these are only ruses, strata-

gems, to win her over. As for women gamblers, they're
probably lesbians. They try to seduce her, too, but take
advantage of their common female condition. Fortune
sometimes prefers them because they're more expressive,
more expansive. They shout "bingo!" ardently; they laugh
and carry on. There's no trace of that oppressive seriousness
that the male gambler is prey to; solitary, stubborn in his
silent combat against that beautiful, evasive woman who
depends on nothing and no one . . . that indiscriminate flirt.
(But it's also possible that our mute pleasure has a deeper,
more mysterious, more symbolic dimension.)

After work (I'm an editor of a wretched, mass-produced
weekly magazine), the casino, with its fluffy carpets, bright
lights, ornate chandeliers and wide-screen TVs in every
corner of the room, feels like home to me. Like home or a
brothel. (In the sixteenth century they used to call gambling
houses "Temples of Pleasure": sacred and secret, like all
pleasures. These were the luxurious casinos found in the hot
springs or spas throughout Europe.) There, I feel comfortable, protected and sheltered from the world. The wait-
resses glide gently by, serve drinks, smile at the familiar
players, replace the pens, and have a kind word for the
winners. As long as I remain in the gambling parlor, loung-
ing in my seat, the only reality is the regular beat of the
counting and the drip of the monotonous numbers far from
all conflict, all worry. Suffering, death, hatred, none of these
exist there; only the buying and selling of boards, as if it
were some strange, marginal Eden. *Eleven. Six. Twenty-
two. Eighty. Nineteen. Thirty-two. Seventy-seven. Twelve.
Forty-four. Thirty-nine.* "Line, we have a line," says the
announcer's metallic voice. She reads the winning numbers
and then adds: "We'll continue until someone gets bingo."
Economy and ritual demand clear and repetitive formulas.

All I need is number fifteen until I get a line. It'll show up right away or it won't be called until the end of the game. Chance . . . that unpredictable order. *"Only in gambling does nothing depend on nothing,"* wrote Dostoevsky. Everything else in the world, hurricanes and blizzards, diseases, the end of love affairs, inheritances, credit ratings, industrial crises, the results of a soccer game or elections, wars, romances, weddings, all can be analyzed, predicted, understood. The progression of numbers, however, is unpredictable, random, surprising. If I wait impatiently for number two to show, no calculation, no combination, no promise, no pact will hurry its appearance. Holding my breath, shaking with anticipation, pen poised, I can only wait trustingly, or despair uneasily. Waiting in silence. I like the silence of gambling halls. Temples and gambling halls are the only places where man, that insignificant charlatan, that senseless gabber, that shameless bigmouth, that banal philosopher, that propagator of lies, that narcissistic braggart, keeps quiet.

Lucia, my psychoanalyst—one of the few people who knows about my love of gambling—once said to me:

"You like the silence of the casinos because you're fed up with the chit-chat of the newspapers and magazines. You should think about changing your profession."

We should all change our profession sometime, Lucia. The doctor, who after twenty years of treating heart attacks, comas, cancers, colon obstructions, feels nothing but indifference in the face of pain and death; the professor who doubts his own knowledge or the possibility of transmitting any kind of it; the secretary who no longer feels revulsion for the company's secrets; the revolutionary who is tired of history; the delegate who is obligated by his party to vote "yes"; the housewife who's raised four kids and a husband, whose only distraction is the little bit of fun she gets feeding the slot machines on her way back from the store. We should also change cities, parents, children, friends, lovers.

"Aren't you tired?" I asked Lucia.

"A little less than you are," she answered. "I don't need to forget my profession in casinos."

9 27 16 90 88 40 44 21 11 17 19 52 60

You should see how often forty-four comes up; it turns up at the beginning in every game. Twenty-seven, though, is fickle. It appears and disappears arbitrarily without mercy toward the player.

I stick my hand in my pocket and pull out another dollar. Special game. Boards double their value. All right. If I win this game not only will I recover all my losses but I'll come out a little ahead.

I buy five boards. For the hell of it, I look for number sixteen. If I don't get it, I decide I'm going to lose. First number, twenty-eight. Yes, I have that one. I jot down three numbers in a row on the same board, but then the numbers shift and begin a new line on other boards. (In life, Claudia, no two games are alike; no one ever played the same trick twice; no one ever wins two games in a row with the same board; no one knows the next combination; there are no two identical beings in the world.)

I don't win that round, or any of the next ones. At two-thirty in the morning, exhausted, I wait anxiously for the last two games. My bones ache, my eyes sting, and I've smoked too much. The worst part of it is that when I get back to my apartment, I'm too agitated to sleep. Since I have to go to work in the morning (at that important magazine that adorns every waiting room, doctor's office, and hair salon), I take a sleeping pill. When I wake up, I'll be struck by remorse: "I've gambled away too much money; I haven't won a cent, and, what's more, I'm somnambulent, depressed, and my body's a wreck.

Still, in spite of all my good intentions, I'll probably be here tomorrow, this cozy temple, scraping the bottom of my pockets, hanging on to that series of numbers, the white balls that leap out of the drum at random. Last night, in the final game, sixteen never showed up.

2

In some casinos, after the final game is played out, when the frustrated players quit, the uniformed employees (both men and women) line up in two rows in the lobby and salute the clients with a slight nod of the head. This small tribute restores the morale of the losers. They are treated like ladies and gentlemen, for only ladies and gentlemen lose money for pleasure.

At three o'clock in the morning this night of chance comes to an end; the spell is finally broken. Each person promptly resumes his conventional role, of good citizen, father or mother of a family, bureaucrat, or journalist (like me). The vast majority, I'm sure, won't say a word about how and where they've spent the evening, or night, or wee hours of the morning. Or maybe they'll make up some alibi: "I had to work late," or "A client showed up unexpectedly," or "I ran into a guy I went to school with," or "I had dinner with an old pal." Gambling, like masturbation, is a solitary vice, unspeakable, a secret that must be kept to oneself.

Like armored beetles, a line of taxis waits outside the entranceway of the casino. The players hurriedly jump in. The city (outside the temple walls, the brothel, the house of vice), is silent, bright, and empty like an abandoned movie theater.

Under a bunch of old newspapers a short distance from the entranceway sleeps a beggar, distant, indifferent to this game of chance. Walking by him, I can't help but feel a slight twinge of guilt.

3

"At first," I tell my psychoanalyst, "I considered slot machine players to be mediocre, worthless people: your ordinary housewife with obscure frustrations and impossible dreams, throwing away the coins she saved at the market; or men with no futures and no jobs, who squander their time in bars; or old retirees with no family; or other marginal characters."

"When did your opinion about slot machine players change?" Lucia asks me ingenuously.

In Latin Lucia means *light*. I wonder if her mother had this in mind when she named her. When Lucia took up this profession, she surely must have realized how apt it was.

"When I started gambling," I tell her. "Listen, I'm not unemployed, or retired, or living on the fringes, or a frustrated housewife. In the beginning," I add, "it was only a pastime, a distraction. I used to go down to the corner bar, order a coffee, and toss a couple of coins into the slot machine, just out of curiosity. But soon," I explain, "it turned into something else. I noticed the change when I realized that what was important for me wasn't breakfast anymore or reading the newspaper while leaning against the bar, but whether the machine was occupied or not so I could play. I stood watch over her, I stalked her, and if some other guy was playing the machine when I entered the bar, I felt annoyed, unsatisfied. Then I would wait for my rival to lose so that I could take over. It wasn't just a matter of playing for a few coins; I was after the big prize. I wasn't after the money itself—the compensation was not in proportion to the investment—I was out to conquer her, to win.

" 'Come on,' I say to the glittering machine in the bar. 'You and I know each other, ol' girl. You have a plan, a secret, and I'm going to uncover it. I'm stronger than you are. Sing! Sing, little princess. Let go your fountain of coins, your golden spurt. Be a good girl, have multiple orgasms. Women are more generous than men: they nourish, give birth, protect, and console. Men aren't very generous. We give a little semen, that's it. We don't like to give and we don't like to be asked to give. We have to be trained hard to give what little we do. The only thing we have plenty of is power. But I'm not allowed to force you, little girl. I can't break you open to make you give me something. I have to respect the rules of the game. I can't rape you. I have to warm you up first by slipping in a few coins; a little foreplay. Like a client with a prostitute.'

"I've devoted myself to a serious study of the symptoms of these machines," I explain to the psychoanalyst. "When they heat up, when they get cold, when they start to throb, the frequency of the music, the combination of the figures."

"You've noticed, of course," observed Lucia, "that the word *figure* is used when describing a woman's body?"

20

"Nor have I failed to notice," I confirm, "that they could just as easily have called them *slut machines*. They have a hole, and I fill it literally up with coins."

"Whom do you want to penetrate? Whom do you want to impregnate? Whom do you want to reciprocate?" the psychoanalyst interrogates me. "In this case the metaphor doesn't hold. *Slut* can mean *prostitute;* but it's a prostitute who sometimes denies you pleasure, right? Even though you've allowed her to swallow all your money, she doesn't always gratify you. You want to seduce her, dominate her, but in reality she's the one who dominates you; she's the one who shows her autonomy, her independence."

"Your interpretation is not very original," I tell the psychiatrist. "In almost every language the terminology of love and seduction is also used in reference to gambling and war. Siege, conquest, penetration, resistance, attack, assault, sword, bomb, missile, engagement, alliance, defense."

"Your gambling problem is not very original either," Lucia responds. "You're constantly making references to Dostoevsky when you could just as well have quoted the local tailor or the soldier's widow who suffer the same addiction."

"The desire to gamble never ends," I confess to Lucia. "It ends temporarily each night at closing time, but starts again the next day. You wait for opening time like a horse waiting for the finish line at the beginning of a race. If you lose, you play again because you've lost and if you win, you play again because you've won."

"So you've found the fountain of unquenchable desire," Lucia comments sarcastically. "The only limit is exhaustion, closing time, or lack of money, right? Sure," she quickly adds, "a casino is more accessible than a woman: it's always open for business; there will always be a table waiting

21

for you; you'll always receive smiles when you come and go. Just like a brothel. But women who aren't in the brothel demand more than money, and they're not always at your disposal."

"If you're referring to Claudia," I venture (I don't like it when the psychoanalyst surprises me with an interpretation that hasn't already occurred to me), "I was a gambler long before I met her." (I was already gambling when I was going out with Claudia. I gambled before our dates and I gambled after them. Our meetings and separations made me extremely anxious. Sometimes, while she slept after making love, I would sneak off to the closest casino and start to play, so that I could concentrate on myself; as though I had to flee from this feeling of alienation of a body that got too close, from a "me" that was excessively symbolic. Gambling soothed me. I never told her; gambling was my last redoubt against the invasion of love.)

"Of course," Lucia responds, "you were already gambling at that time, and you were hiding your affliction even from Claudia. In that way, you felt more protected and could easily forgive yourself. I'm sure she feels more charitable toward the vice of gambling than of infidelity."

"It's curious," I confirm. "Claudia thought I was a womanizer, not a gambler."

"You did nothing to clear up that misunderstanding," Lucia points out implacably.

"Gambling only creates problems for me," I say. "Promiscuity creates problems for others too. In this economy of conflicts, gambling is less dangerous."

"Now you've found a virtue in it!" Lucia exclaims contemptuously. "However, it's about time you listen to yourself a little when you're not gambling, and this is a good place to do it."

22

It's true. In that small discreetly carpeted office, with that delicate feminine touch of dried flower arrangements and books stacked neatly in the bookcase, I am able to listen to myself. Talking to oneself in the internal whirlwind is not the same as listening all ears to oneself in the serenity and silence of an office isolated from time and space. Private consulting rooms are like airports: they float; they are nowhere. This lack of coordinates allows us to hear ourselves better. I am, therefore, paying to hear myself.

"It's a lot better than paying to hear the chant of numbers in a bingo game," Lucia said, in the beginning, and I had to force myself to forgive the sarcasm.

One of the things I like best about this psychoanalyst is that she smokes. She's not beyond good and evil. She absorbs her patients' anxiety, makes it her own and, like them, smokes. Even though some of her patients hate smoke, she still smokes. That makes her more vulnerable, more human. She smokes, writes, takes notes; this puts us almost on an equal plane.

"I have the impression," she says, "that you substituted the desire for Claudia with the desire for gambling."

"Gambling," I reply, "is a kind of vertigo that I only experienced with Claudia in bed. Neither one of us wanted to be the first to confess our exhaustion; that would have been humiliating. It was as if we were both thinking: 'I'll make love until the other cries "enough." ' It never happened though. We both wanted to be more insatiable than the other."

"Why was there something to prove?" Lucia asks, playing naive. (I don't trust her. I know it's a strategy.)

"To exceed the limit," I struggle to say.

"To exceed the limit," Lucia repeats. I suppose that when she repeats one of my sentences, it's to make me more conscious of it. "What did you both think was beyond the limit?" she asks.

"The pleasure was in crossing the limit," I say as my head begins to hurt.

"When you're gambling and you win, do you quit or do you keep playing?" she interrogates.

"I keep playing," I confess, drowsily.

"So there, too, it's a question of surpassing the limit," Lucia deduces.

"Claudia never played a single game of cards, never set foot inside a casino," I answer miserably, as if that could refute her interpretation.

"At least you've proven that you can play at something else," she concludes.

I leave the session furious and in a foul mood. I'd like to kick something, throw a rock through a window, set off a fire alarm, rob a bank. The lofty image I have of myself keeps me from grabbing some woman's ass. Since I'm not going to grab some woman's ass, I spit violently at the curb.

"Pig," a fat woman says as she passes me.

"Cow," I answer back.

And to think that a night at the magazine awaits me. What's on the menu for this week? Ah, the little prince has fractured his collarbone while on a ski trip. Will the flamenco dancer get her divorce or not? The daughter of the Secretary of Commerce was caught in a disco without underwear. The tennis champion has hooked up with an American model. A television announcer is going to work for another station. Smuggled cocaine seized in Persian rugs. Earthquake in Guatemala. Your weekly horoscope—

Scorpio: "Don't take any foolish risks with your money."
(Damn it.)

If casinos are like brothels, so are psychoanalysts' offices and so is the magazine's editorial room.

4

he passionate gambler's imperturbability, like a lover's, is a symptom of obsession more stubborn than others. A person who screams, carries on, and throws a tantrum may actually be more free than another who is so strict with his passion, he doesn't allow even a gesture to get in the way between him and his dependence. While I loved Claudia, as impetuous as I am, I still appeared to be a cold, enigmatic lover. Never a premature ejaculation, never an awkward, uncontrolled caress. Oh how I hid my spasms, my trembling, my jealousy, my obsession. I seemed cold, self-sufficient, like the gambler missing just one number on his board, but who shows not a single expression to betray it. I think it was then—while I was in love with Claudia—that I started to gamble again. I played before we went out. I played after we made love. I played at night in casinos if she had fallen asleep and, I, an insomniac, couldn't get to sleep. I gambled when she went on vacation with her family, but I also gambled if we went together.

I have noticed an obscure melancholy in those who have given up a vice, a passion. It's the nostalgia for a dependency that reveals our weakness, our vulnerability. Take those who say they've given up smoking, for example. I look at their mouths and they seem singularly deprived. They are castrated mouths without a phallus. They have become severe. These converts look disapprovingly at people like me who light up a cigarette in a public place: we contribute to air pollution, we traffic in carbon dioxide, we expose ourselves to cancer and heart disease. How wild and delirious we addicted gamblers must seem, staring at those white balls as they spin chaotically from the drums, while some employee in a red uniform, sick of this stupid game, reads the numbers in a frigid, monotone voice (the arbitrary voice of God?).

Liberated from an absolute God whom we consider the fraud of uncultured ignoramuses, we give ourselves over to the cult of demi-gods: sex, money, narcissism, gambling. No one ever really becomes a true atheist.

5

ast year I took a train to Baden-Baden. I watched the countryside through the window. Beside the track huge, gray cement factories had been erected, like giant monoliths, with their tubular intestines exposed, their cylindrical phalluses pointing toward the low sky, the missiles of an economic war that exploded a long time ago. Many are no longer functioning, but no one bothers to demolish them. There they stand, abandoned, like enormous idols, mini-deities of a vain and destructive civilization, whose dark purpose future civilizations will try to decipher.

Before reaching the border, the vegetation looks poor and depressing, like the fossilized fruit of an old menopausal womb. The bald, ash-colored mountains look like squeezed lemons.

The train passed through a dark tunnel and reappeared under a colorless sky. The rotten smell from the paper and synthetic textile factories occasionally reached even into our closed compartment. Just imagine, we write on and dress ourselves in this manufactured putrefaction.

I walked the streets of Baden-Baden parsimoniously until I found the casino. It was an elegant, old turn-of-the-century salon with heavy chandeliers and striped purple carpets. The well-preserved crimson curtains are just as they were when Dostoevsky used to gamble here. Probably no one would visit the old casino anymore if there weren't posters all over the place recalling the Russian author's passion, his frenzy for gambling. Now at the end of this century, with the triumph of the consumer, there are customers for everything. People who have never even read Dostoevsky and never will have their pictures taken in the old casino's vestibule, under a daguerreotype of the author or a commemorative plaque. I, too, am a customer. I consume memories, illusions, fantasies, like everyone. Those who come here to the Baden-Baden casino buy, for a hundred marks, something more than roulette chips. They buy prestige, a legend, the illusion of a romantic past. The chips are made of mother-of-pearl, as they were in the last century. I get real pleasure from touching them, having them in my pocket. I love those few casinos that, not having yielded to the Yankee ethics, still use the pinkish mother-of-pearl chips. For each player, a different color; for every number, a different chip. I remember Anaïs—a beautiful European emigrant from the New World—who kept a pearl chip of every color inside her black silk stockings, near her lace garters. Blue: one thousand marks; gold: five thousand. And that magnificent orangish chip, shining like the sun at dawn: a hundred thousand.

"You can see yourself reflected in these little mirrors," Anaïs once remarked, and I suppose this kind of dreamy speculation enabled her to tolerate the boredom of her native Rio de la Plata; a coastal town filled with poor émigrés and persecuted anarchists.

The director of the Baden-Baden casino made himself available for a brief interview. He is a small, polite man who runs the casino like a museum, knowing well that its greatest attraction is its faithfulness to the past. I ask him if the great European fortunes still flow in the way they used to.

"No, sir," he replies courteously. "Today the great fortunes are made anonymously—in the stock market, not in the casino. We have democratized." I notice a slight irony in his words: clandestine fortunes, illegal money, and the like.

Reluctantly, he had computers installed in the vestibule to comply with international game regulations. The bettor must present his or her identity card upon entering. Two thousand gamblers have been denied entrance.

"It's a little offensive," he tells me in confidence. "My employees can recognize regular clients instantly. The others," he adds, "the occasional gamblers, are harmless. None of them would hurt the casino. Before," he concludes, "people wanted to be recognized for who they were; now they are proud to have identification papers, credit cards, computerized plastic."

I ask him if he's seen many writers in the casino lately.

"No, sir," he replies. "Many tennis players, soccer players, businessmen, actors, representatives. The name 'Dostoevsky' sounds familiar to them, but they don't know why. That's all that matters though. They don't bet much. They just come to have their picture taken under Dostoevsky's daguerreotype. The photograph is compliments of the casino," he adds, his face expressionless.

The interview is for a flashy Spanish tourist magazine.

Glossy paper, gorgeous photography, beautiful landscapes, with the most expensive ads in the market: liquor, fine watches, designer clothes, sophisticated sports cars. Catlike models between sheets, exclusive designer jewelry set against canvases of famous painters who died, of course, of cold and hunger in those days when people still died for art, when painting and writing were forms of heroism and mysticism.

Jaime, the director, went to college with me. When he was young, he founded a leftist magazine, the kind that got every issue out on the street only after a thousand obstacles and with the help of an army of volunteers, from printers to vendors. The magazine was the voice of a generation, but after twenty years it went broke. Those days of mimeographing copies in the middle of the night between drinks of strong coffee, rushed sex behind the huge reels of paper, and philosophical discussions in the bathroom have come to an end. Later, a minister—a former colleague on the faculty—named Jaime director of the tourist magazine. Jaime reinvented himself. Now he wears designer suits, he's bought a speed boat, keeps expensive mistresses, organizes cruises on the Pacific, and carries a leather Cartier wallet for his numerous credit cards. The magazine is quite beautiful; it could easily be an art magazine. The ministry sends free copies to the big hotels, executive waiting rooms, airports, famous specialists' offices, and high-class private clubs.

I sold the article to Jaime only because I wanted to go to Baden-Baden.

Dostoevsky writes that sometimes in those sumptuous rooms of the casino decorated with opulent, fringed chandeliers and gold-edged tables, the muffled sound of a pistol shot could be heard.

*

Across the street, beneath a dark glass marquee and golden gothic letters, is the pawnshop, looking perhaps much the way it did a century ago. This is where Dostoevsky got his gambling money in exchange for his wife's few jewels and furniture from her dowry. He never pawned a manuscript, though. They wouldn't have given him anything for it.

There are hardly any more pawnshops left. Now there are banks. We don't pawn jewelry or family furniture: we mortgage our days, our hours of work, our freedom, our joy. Joy? In a world where usefulness is the only value, joy is useless . . . except for enjoying.

"It's a game for idiots," comments one of the regulars sitting at the bar while I throw coins into the slot machine. The pictures appear and disappear (the pear, the apple, the strawberry, two maraschino cherries, the bar of gold, a plum) on the lighted screen, conforming to the invisible program of a tiny chip that vibrates like a neuron.

"You're throwing your money away! You'll never win," the regular insists, not taking his eyes off me. I wonder if he really wishes to play but is afraid of losing. He doesn't know that in order to win, you have to lose.

"You don't play to win money, pal," I answer him. He looks at me, stupefied.

"Then what do you play for?"

"For pleasure," I say and put in another coin.

Anyway, like Dostoevsky, when I lose a lot of money, I'm tormented by regret. Not only with respect to the beggars and drop-outs, the poor, and the sick, but with respect to myself. Like the great Russian writer, I don't possess my own fortune, or the possibility of inheriting or obtaining one by those secret, speculative means so popular nowadays. The money I make every month is from my work at the magazine; exhausting, competitive, and even envied as it is. I have never been rich, nor will I ever be, but I'm almost forty and have a stable career. "Too old to voluntarily renounce anything," I say to myself. "Especially a vice." At forty, all is allowed, because in some way, all is lost.

But Dostoevsky knew well that a gambler has regrets only after he's lost; never after he's won or has the hope of winning.

6

No city could be more boring than St. Petersburg. What was Dostoevsky to do there, burdened with debts, hounded by his stupid family whom he supported? Flee to Baden-Baden, leaving his young wife, Anna Grigorievna, in Dresden. He needs money and a passion to absorb him. But back in those days, Baden-Baden was just as boring as St. Petersburg and as depressing as Berlin.

Dostoevsky, a brilliant, nervous man, never found an activity that was sufficiently consuming to vent his intelligence, his enthusiasm, his energy, his thirst for the absolute. He had already proven that he was superior to Tolstoy and Turgenev. Tolstoy, like Balzac, was a "robust writer," that is, someone able to write a five-hundred-page novel without revealing his subjectivity, his own anguish in a single sentence. These writers wrote the same way painters paint frescoes or murals. Look to them for period pieces, history, not dreams, or delirium, or fantasies. Dostoevsky, on the other hand, wrote about the interior, that part of us which makes us dizzy if we get too close. Those who go deeply into themselves experience at some specific moment a kind of intoxication of the intelligence and the senses, what's called *le vertige des grandes profondeurs*. Dostoevsky was familiar with it; he could only live on the surface for a short time, just long enough to be able to reimmerse himself. Dostoevsky gets married, but he cannot be a good husband. The sweet, young Anna Grigorievna, who carries around a diary full of trivialities, hardly stimulates him. He flees to Baden-Baden to throw himself into an all-consuming passion—gambling. Besides, this way he can feel guilty enough (he loses all his money, hocks Anna's jewels, the family furniture, and even his own coat) to love her again, to feel remorse, and to long for her.

Some people can love only if they feel guilty.

I've taken a loan out from the bank. Now I am an indebted man. Now I can fall in love.

A letter from Dostoevsky to Anna (in his raptures of guilt he calls her *Annushka*): "I have lost more than my means will allow."

After an intensely exhilarating night in the Baden-Baden casino (at midnight he had won a fortune; three hours later he lost it all, along with Anna's earrings), Dostoevsky writes in his diary: "In every part of my life I have exceeded the limits."

7

The first slot machine was invented by a fellow named Charles Fey from San Francisco. He called it the "Liberty Bell" and secretly had it installed in his gambling house. Later he went to Chicago and manufactured more of them, each with a different design, but all from the same mold: a box decorated with colored lights and a sound like a cash register. Liberty Bell—nice name. Lights and music: an infantile inducement, no doubt, but quite effective. It takes us back to childhood when we were dazzled by handkerchiefs and rabbits pulled from a top hat. In these new Pandora's boxes, the handkerchiefs are strawberries; the rabbits, apples, and at some point the winning combination clicks to let loose a waterfall of coins. "Shower of Gold," one Spanish manufacturer named his slot machine.

" 'Shower of Gold' also refers to a sexual service advertised in the newspapers," I tell the psychoanalyst. *"Cas-*

cade, stream, orgasm: the similarity is not exactly mysterious."

"If it were, there wouldn't be so many addicts," the psychoanalyst confirms.

"But in casinos, money circulates frenetically, from hand to hand, from one person to another like desire, which alights for an instant and then vanishes."

"Maybe the gambler would like to hold on to it," Lucia interprets. "He dreams of winning *all* the money, *every* game, to quench his desire for playing once and for all."

"Desire is exhausting," I acknowledge.

"But giving up desire makes you sick," Lucia states. "Psychoanalysts' offices are full of such sick people," she says.

When I left the session I stopped for coffee at the nearest bar. There was a blond slot machine inside, all dolled up, whistling a little jingle. But I ignored it.

"One isn't obliged to desire *all* the time," Lucia told me as I was leaving her office. "The truth is, sometimes it's comforting, relaxing, nice not to desire."

8

work for a very well-known magazine. It's one of those sensationalist, widely circulated, full-color magazines with a lot of pictures and little text. You can find it in every hair parlor (from local barber shop to high-class salon) and in every supermarket between the fried tomatoes and the plastic gloves. You'll see it in waiting rooms, in your doctor's office, your dentist's office, and at your attorney's office. Triviality is a grand leveler; everyone reads this stuff: the queen and her servants, the bank director and his clients, the members of parliament and the electorate. Year after year, consistently it clings to the top of the sales charts.

What does it sell? It sells scandals, exclusives on celebrity weddings, nude shots of anonymous and noteworthy people, jet crashes and natural disasters, new ways to lose weight or prolong your life, change your face, your partner, your career. But above all it sells tits and ass. As if it were aimed at a far-sighted audience, the photographs are enormous, "eloquent." The voice doesn't speak, nor do the words; it's the image that speaks. We've published the world's most famous tits and ass; hormone-injected tits and sagging tits; tits like peaches, tits like pears; authentic tits and doctored tits; barrel asses and narrow asses; asses in profile and asses straight on; asses of singers, of actresses, of mothers and daughters; of grandmothers and granddaughters; management asses and cabaret dancers' asses. Whores' tits and lesbians' tits, even tits of transvestites. Everything that has been hidden and locked away for so long jumps out, explodes to the surface, hypertrophied. Silicone boobs, drooping boobs, rejuvenated boobs, red nipples, purple nipples, brown nipples, blue nipples; shaved pubic hair, pubes with metallic stars, triangular pubes, oval, concave or convex. We also sell "exotic sex," "picturesque sex," for weary, bored Western bodies, sick of seeing themselves reflected in other similar bodies; bodies pale like theirs, flabby like theirs, satiated with proteins and carbohydrates like theirs. Young people from the Third World, brown-skinned men and women with dark shining eyes, thick fleshy lips, wide noses, jutting cheekbones, and, beneath their tropical clothing, a swollen sex. Sometimes I write the captions below these photographs. Conventional and ephemeral prose, full of the commonplace—"The mysterious spell of other bodies, other geographies." "The passionate look of a she-wolf in heat." "The enchantment of brown skin." In a separate column, there's a list of the travel agencies offering air transportation, hotel and sexual services at affordable prices: Taiwan, Paraguay, Bolivia, the Philippines.

I've got my own office, phone, fax, copier, word processor, secretary, phone with a direct line to the boss's office (the fat hypochondriac) and an open account to buy exclusives. I also have a couple of novice reporters at my disposal, fresh out of college, ready (if they want to move up the ladder) to execute any task, no matter how low or ridiculous. ("Subservience is more important than efficiency," is the motto they were taught from cradle through high school and college.)

I barricade myself behind the computer, facing the table full of photographs, papers, long fax sheets. And, from the back of my desk drawer, I extract a deck of French cards with red diamonds, black clubs, and bleeding hearts. Last night, before falling asleep, I learned a new game of solitaire from a book on cards. I'm going to try it.

The secretary knocks on my office door. She has a humble way of knocking when on a mission of her own and a deliberate way of knocking when on a mission for the boss. The boss sends her when he's in a foul mood and wishes to maintain distance and reserve between us.

"Come in," I signal to Flora, while I look for my favorite suit in solitaire.

"The boss wants you to go to San Sebastian," Flora informs me. "I've already reserved your ticket."

"Do you like diamonds or hearts better?" I ask her while I lay out a row of cards on the desk.

"You'd just better go to his office right away; he's in a bad mood. Plus his ribs hurt," the secretary says.

"The left or the right?" I ask without moving. "If it's the left," I add, "pleurisy; the right, gas. So, another terrorist interview?"

"I think so," Flora answers and she blushes because she doesn't like to be disloyal to the boss or to see me playing cards.

"I should have picked hearts," I tell her and show her a

sanguine-colored five. "You can keep playing if you want," I say sarcastically.

I cross the room full of desks and nervous people busy answering telephones, consulting newspapers and magazines, calling agencies, reading long faxes, and barking back and forth at one another. We're the cutting edge, no doubt about it. The *cutting edge*: as noisy as it is hollow; as brilliant as it is fatuous. The cutting edge gets dulled in a single day.

It turns out that it's the left side that ails the boss.

"I must have caught the flu," he says. His health—which he believes to be extremely fragile—is a sore point between us, like exclusives, feature reports, and photos. It's a rule . . . every Wednesday, the day we close, he thinks he's sick.

"It's strange," I say cautiously. "You don't go out much. You just go from the magazine to your house, from your house to a restaurant, and always by car."

"I must have caught cold last night in the living room," he diagnoses, quite distraught. "I stayed up watching a movie until one o'clock and my wife turned off the heat. She said it was getting too hot."

"Hot flashes, no doubt," I remarked, trying to distract him with someone else's suffering. "But your color's good. You don't look sick," I assure him.

"We'll see," he replies incredulously. "I think I've got a fever. But you," he adds, raising his voice, "you've got to go to San Sebastian. We got the interview. It's cost me a lot of time and money. So hurry up and go and call me when you get there. I'll be waiting."

Flora left the hearts and diamonds on the table just as I had dealt them. There they are, like wilted flowers with their dark prophecy.

"In the olden days," I tell the psychoanalyst a short time later, "numbers were part of religion. They were magical symbols to be interpreted like the movement of the stars, the viscera of animals, and the flight of birds. Seven, for example, was a sacred number, as was three. They didn't mean only one thing, but several things and their meanings multiplied in relation to each other. Perhaps," I venture, "gambling is a displaced manifestation of this religious sentiment."

"No doubt," she says. "But that origin doesn't justify your addiction, just as religious fervor doesn't justify fanaticism or bigotry. We're not concerned with trying to discover your subjective motives for gambling. If you're interested in numbers anthropologically, write an article. That's not *our* business here."

Transform your subjective passion into something else: that was what Dostoevsky did after Baden-Baden.

I wonder if I'm capable of such a sublimation.

"I have to go to San Sebastian for work," I tell Lucia.

"For detoxification a change of environment doesn't hurt," the psychoanalyst says, "even though you'd have to abstain for a longer period than that."

"I'm not really sure I want to," I say sincerely.

"Sometimes one doesn't know what one wants," she says.

Wisdom, according to the Orientals, is an absence of desires. A strict discipline, a withdrawal from the world to eliminate every desire. But I am in the world. What's more, I make my living off being *cutting edge*.

"*Bon voyage,*" Lucia says at the end of the session; her farewell fortifies me.

The art of endings: a good writer and a good psychoanalyst should know how to master the art of separation: how to suspend the reader until the next page and the

42

patient until the next session. It has to be an ending that doesn't interrupt the seduction, that leaves it floating, because if this suspension is ineffective, he could wind up with no reader, or no patient. In this, as in everything, it concerns the art of seduction, perhaps the only art in this world.

In games, each turn is called a "partida" or "round." There are rounds of poker, chess, bingo, bridge, roulette, and card games. I reflect on the term. "Partida" sometimes means *escape,* sometimes a *separation.* What am I separated from? What is it I want to get close to? What am I fleeing from? What do I hope to find? The orgasmic moment of triumph. Some invoke it with a quiet prayer: "twenty-eight . . . twenty-eight . . . twenty-eight." Others fling their boards on the floor and fix their eyes on the TV screen where, pompously, deliberately, the balls appear.

Salvador, a player of great renown (for his arrogance in the face of luck) was able just to glance at a new board and memorize its fifteen numbers instantaneously. Later he would return his boards, light a cigarette, and listen to the monotonous chant of the numbers, taking no notes. He never failed. He would shout "line" or "bingo" relying only on his photographic memory. This skill disheartened his fellow players, and Salvador intuitively knew that the psychological effect on others was the best way to summon luck.

What I like best about my profession is the lack of sedentariness. One day I'm in Barcelona, the next I'm in Paris, and the next in London. I grab a small bag and from that moment on I feel light, almost weightless . . . a being in transit, who quickly sheds his past and whose future flies along with him. I like hotel life. Just as in airports, one is always passing through. It's a floating space, without tradition, without history, without roots. It doesn't matter where you were born or who your parents are. In hotels, a Swiss person speaks with a Brit, an Andalucian with a Catalan, an American with an Arab.

I took a plane to San Sebastian. I ended the interview as quickly as possible—a political terrorist, drunk with heroism and ideological tics; you've seen one, you've seen them all. I decided to make the most of hotel life and the fact that I was a man passing through. (The bill was paid and I was free from bothersome acquaintances.) It was an English hotel, stately and decadent, with white balustrades and blossoming tamarinds. Formerly it was frequented by the idle rich but now, in contrast, accommodates a triumphant bourgeoisie of dubious tastes.

In the middle of the lobby stood an old, black grand piano. At sundown, when twilight settles in and they begin to light the elegant lanterns on the promenade—capped like old-fashioned ladies—the pianist, a tall gray-haired man in his fifties, softly and reservedly plays nostalgic tunes from the forties, like a survivor from a lost era. A dinosaur.

The Kursal casino is a step away from the old hotel, but I wasn't lured by it. I felt comfortable in my white linen pants, my canvas shoes, pink shirt, and blue blazer. Like many women, I occasionally, only occasionally, hang my narcissism on my physique. (Why not say *body*? A man has a *physique*; a woman has a *body*. The linguistic distinction, consecrated by use, reveals the masculine rejection of being considered an object, and the sadistic pleasure of attributing this condition to women.)

I had decided not to gamble, and with that decision my self-esteem rose considerably. I was a free man, no vices. I thought of Dostoevsky. While gambling like a possessed maniac, like a madman (is there any other way to gamble?) by night, and suffering violent bouts of remorse by day, Dostoevsky wrote the dramatic pages of *The Idiot*. Gambling and writing: two intense, obsessive, all-consuming activities. Compulsively drawn to the roulette wheel, where he lost, won, and lost again, caught up in the whirlwind of impossible dreams (no one can win what he really wants), Dostoevsky played until closing time, and later, without skipping a beat, without needing to rest, he set about writing the world's most compassionate book. Two feverish activities, two forceful channels of energy that bubbled and boiled, and when they finally burst, shook the universe. The froth of passion. During this period of exuberant vigor, he could have also been a splendid lover, but the sweet, tiny, tender Annushka never understood her husband's excesses, and he feared hurting her. A man who could have inseminated an entire city! (Someone once accused him of trying to molest a girl in a bathroom. His youngest daughter, Sonia, had just died. He was desperate. For a man of his temperament, any expression—even tenderness—is libidinal. Gambling. Writing. Loving his own daughter.)

I cozied up in a worn-out, red leather armchair, surrounded by English prints of fox hunts and shipwrecks. Elegant, pale old ladies with dusty cheeks drank cups of aromatic tea and spoke in whispering voices. The few men in the room were old as well, gentlemen who trembled uncontrollably from Parkinson's disease (which awaits us all in old age, like a humiliation), and whose gazes were lost in the shadows of the sea at dusk.

Suddenly, like a raid on the elegant, moribund landscape of the hotel, a tall, very thin girl with long, straight hair down to her waist strolled in. She was young, dynamic, agile and addressed the hotel employees with a spontaneity and familiarity that did not seem owing exclusively to an affinity of age. I smiled. What was this gust of youth doing in the calm, senile ambiance of an English hotel for pensioners? She sat down at the bar and, joking with the waiter, ordered a gin-fizz. At that moment the piano man was playing "Stormy Weather"; one of my favorites. Music is always a good way to start a conversation. She had looked at me cheekily (I adore provocative women) so I approached the bar. She'd never heard "Stormy Weather." The truth was, she told me, she preferred rock. All that romantic music, she added, seemed a little passé.

"I'm probably a little passé too," I confessed.

"Come on," she said naively. "You can't be over thirty-four."

"Leopardi says death is the mother of fashion," I cited.

"Who's Leopardi? A soccer player? I hate soccer."

Her name was Magda. She didn't like the hotel. She found it old and decadent, but her father stayed there two months out of the year, and she was visiting him to hit him up for money. Her father was wealthy—he owned a chain of shoe stores—but he was extremely stingy. She asked me what I did for a living and I told her I was a reporter. She thought that was great, really cool, though she didn't say why. She would like to have been a reporter too, though actually, her greatest desire was to be a cartoonist. I confessed that I wasn't an expert in that department. She told me that didn't matter because she, for her part, never read the newspaper. She got all her news from television. She had been enrolled in an English institute once but she was expelled for playing a practical joke on one of the teachers. Punishment that was a bit harsh, but she was glad because ever since then she has felt free. She asked me if I had any coke. I told her no, just cigarettes. She didn't like my brand; she preferred dark tobacco, but finally, she accepted a Lucky. "You'll die if all you do is smoke tobacco," she warned.

As if urging the guests to retire, the waiters were extinguishing the lights in the hall one row at a time. I think the songs from that glossy piano with its yellowed keys were provoking a kind of tickling in the muscular appendage below my abdomen, and I mentally ordered it to calm down.

We men often speak to our member, as if it were a friend or an enemy that shares our body. I suspect women have a less direct relationship with theirs, perhaps because theirs is inside. Ours, on the other hand, is external, a banner, a flag, capricious, selfish, infantile.

Magda told me she'd spent her honeymoon in this hotel two years ago. I was surprised she was married; it wasn't her style.

"This hotel isn't too romantic for you?" I asked.

"My father paid for it; it was his idea. I think he's got a fixation with this place."

If there is one thing I detest in this world, it's a woman telling me her personal problems when a piano is playing and my sex is erect. I don't talk about my work problems in bed. If we were going to exchange secrets, better to get to the point. So I asked her: "You still married?"

She swallowed the last swig of her gin-fizz and answered, "No, of course not. I must have been drunk when I got married."

At last we agreed on something. A man marries only when he's drunk, a woman, only when she's drunk. This coincidence brought new life to my member.

"I like you," I told her.

"I like you too," she told me.

Like is an excellent verb for human relations. It implies the predominance of the senses: I like your skin, your breasts, your mouth, the nape of your neck, your armpits, your pubis, your sex; you like my ears, my cheeks, my chin, my back, my toes, my fingertips, my legs.

We went up to the room, joking as we climbed the stairs. There was a window that opened onto the beach, lit up at that hour by the white lamps on the boardwalk. You could hear the gentle breaking of the waves.

48

She asked me to close the window: she didn't like to screw, she said, to the crashing noise of the waves. Her declaration caused a slight decline in my penis, which is the hypersensitive kind. To help it recover, I tried to take off Magda's clothes, uncover her breasts under her sweater, but she told me she'd rather take her own clothes off; the other way, she said, seemed humiliating. She proposed we undress together in front of the big mirror on the armoire. That wasn't my favorite sport but it didn't seem prudent to argue. While I took off my new white canvas shoes, sitting on the edge of the bed and she, next to me, took off her Havana moccasins, I got the feeling that this was a game between two school chums, as if the two of us (she and I) were roommates taking off our clothes after some graduation ceremony, laughing at each other's toes and back hair. I realized that if this simile went any further, our night of lovemaking was going to be a disaster. Roommates don't turn me on.

When we were finally naked, she led me by the hand in front of the giant oval mirror covering the armoire. Together, we looked like an innocent photograph. Adam and Eve strolling through paradise. But Eve was looking at me with desire.

"You're in good shape," she commented, casting a glance over my naked body. It occurred to me that the ways of lust were infinite, unknown and certainly individual.

"So are you," I echoed stupidly.

The ways of lust are infinite: it didn't seem appropriate to take the initiative. She was a very headstrong, very equal, very determined girl.

"I don't like to rush," she warned.

It was nice to agree on something. Naked, she led me to the bed. We lay down face up and slowly began to caress each other while we smoked the same cigarette. She told me she knew how to smoke through her vagina. Fine. I can play the piano with my dick, like Errol Flynn. She laughed and told me I should hold a public performance in the hotel bar in the morning. I told her I only liked private scandals. I work for a magazine that handles the public ones.

At that moment I remembered an old movie *When the Crowd Roars,* in which Charlton Heston and Eleanor Parker carry on a passionate love affair. ("That typical love-hate thing bores me," Magda said.) I remembered because the screenwriter had Heston compare a woman to a used piano. "More like *well* used," poor Eleanor Parker was made to reply.

"You're either older than you look or you know a lot," Magda said at the exact moment when she decided, in one swift, decisive movement, to switch the traditional mission-ary position—my favorite; I'm conservative. I became the native. She was the missionary and she seemed completely at ease in her role.

Dostoevsky believed there were only two great characters in all literature: his own idiot prince, Michkin, and Don Quixote.

When the dominating missionary and the submissive na-tive simultaneously shared the final eruption—always a du-bious coincidence—Magda asked, "What's your name, any-way?"

"Michkin," I said.

She laughed without understanding.

"Are your parents Russian?"

"No," I said.

Life's best cigarette is the one smoked after making love.

"Sometimes I think I make love just to better enjoy my

cigarette," Magda said. This was another affinity we both shared. The second one just isn't the same. "I've got to go," she muttered, suddenly looking at her wristwatch lying on the floor. "Do you know which floor my father's on?" she asked me hurriedly.

"I don't know your father," I said.

"Oh well, it doesn't matter, I'll find him," Magda said. "Three A.M. is a good time to find him. He doesn't sleep. He's got insomnia," she added.

I watched her from the bed as she quickly got dressed and gathered her things.

"See you soon! You're great!" Magda hollered from the door and blew me a kiss.

I looked at the clock. It was in fact three in the morning. I had one hour before the Kursal closed. One hour . . . enough to lose, enough to win. I groped around for my linen pants. My shirt. My jacket. At least the casino's close to the hotel. The elevator opened languidly onto the lobby. I walked down the hall. The pink light of the Kursal marquee cast a colored glow over my face. I went in. Hiding my tension, I showed my identification documents to the employees at the entrance counter.

"Thank you, sir," they said, returning my papers.

A doorman in a black uniform and a starched white shirt opened the door.

"Black on twenty-four!" was the first announcement I heard, at the table closest to the door.

If I had arrived minutes before, I'd have nailed it. Twenty-four is one of my fixed bets. I sighed, stricken. Now I would have to concentrate, exploit some other opportunity.

I stuck my hand in my jacket pocket to take out my

wallet. First I was going to bet on eighteen red, then on sixteen red. Along with the wallet, I unwittingly pulled out Magda's black silk underwear.

"Thirteen on black," the croupier shouted.

It was here, in this great casino of San Sebastian, where Mata Hari was discovered, identified, and detained for belonging to the French counterintelligence. Gambling was her ruin. When she was detained—magnificent, beautiful, elegantly ironic—she had several expensive chips in her hand. "Gentlemen," she said to the dark political police who had surrounded her, "a good gambler never quits when she's ahead."

I didn't mention Mata Hari to Magda. She might not have known who she was.

10

So," the psychoanalyst says two days later, "you started gambling again in San Sebastian, and you lost," she sums up.

I squirmed in my chair, irritated.

"Sometimes I win," I defend myself.

"But more often you lose," Lucia remarks skeptically. "If people only lost, they wouldn't get hooked on gambling. The illusory fantasy of winning reinforces the habit."

"Norman Mailer," I explain, "speaks of the 'magnificent elation of the winning gambler, who feels touched by the gods.'"

If nothing else, at least psychoanalysis provides me with an intelligent, educated interlocutor, especially in these times of mediocre ambitions and pretentious ignoramuses. An era when intelligence is muffled and lifeless, like a limp prick, because the vast majority (we live under the dictatorship of the *Vast Majority*) live and die without ever using it. To be born, live, and die one need only learn a few mechanical lessons: put a plug in a socket, press a button, manipulate a computer, drive a car, sign a check, obtain credit, watch TV.

"What exactly is this 'magnificent elation' like for you?" Lucia asks.

"A state of grace," I answer quickly. "The divine grace of the ancient Christians that produced miracles or, for the poets, the inspiration that issued from the muses. I experienced it once in Al-Mamounia, the casino in Marrakesh. (In Al-Mamounia, all the gambling tables are blue. Green is a sacred color, the color of Mohammed. Some gamblers go to Marrakesh's casino specifically because, they say, blue inspires them.) For two thousand pesetas I got a lot of dirhams. In one spectacular move I bet them all on seventeen. You know, right? Seventeen is a cursed number for bettors. Seventeen and I had an old debt pending."

No. She doesn't know. She never gambles, at least not on these infantile games of her patients. How could she know that seasoned gamblers, losers that is, feel a strange, dark attraction to seventeen, an aloof, brutal number that almost never comes up?

"I went to Marrakesh to write an article," I tell her, "with Santos, the photographer. Santos had spent the first two days locked up in the hotel paying for exquisite sexual services of both sexes. That's his interpretation of free sex: in the Third World and at the cheapest possible price. While he was getting it on, I went to the casino and, suddenly inspired, I bet everything on seventeen. And that cursed number, which has meant the ruin of so many gamblers, was generous that night: it came up. The Arabs, who are excellent gamblers, did not invent chess for nothing: they had left the seventeen square empty, in acknowledgment of the curse on that number. So mine were the only winning chips on the square. The croupier paid me—a pile of iridescent chips—and congratulated me. The Arabs slapped me on the back. Then, for a few moments, I felt Norman Mailer's 'magnificent elation.' A kind of assuredness, a confidence in myself that elevated me above other gamblers, other men. Without thinking—gods don't need to think—I placed all the chips I'd won on twenty-four. Black and even. Santos, who at that instant had walked into the room and saw what was happening, told me later that the Arab players—highly superstitious, religious men— stopped betting, stood discreetly aside and contemplated my solitary challenge of destiny. The roulette spun, but I was so confident in my intuition I didn't follow its course. Nothing is as simple as luck when one has connected with it. But it is a fragile, intense, fleeting connection. Too fleeting. Twenty-four came up as I had suspected. The Arabs threw out their exclamations of surprise and admiration again. The croupier smiled and extended the very valuable, resplendent ivory chips. Seeing them, Santos implored: 'Let's go, let's go, let's go right now!' I ignored him. The Al-Mamounia casino has no limits. Theoretically one could break the bank. I took everything I'd won and in a decisive gesture placed it on twenty-eight. Black and even. The white ball rolled again. It jumped two or three times over numbers I couldn't see, nor cared to see, so sure was I of my good luck. Then it stopped. I turned around to celebrate my latest triumph with Santos when I heard the metallic, laconic voice of the croupier: *'Le trente-six rouge,'* he said. *'Cinq pleins, demi-plein et trois carrés.'*

"It had landed on thirty-six," I continued, "a red, feminine number I detest and never bet on. I prefer black. In my arrogance, I hadn't noticed that when I placed my entire winnings on twenty-eight, the Arab gamblers, who'd been abstaining, replaced their bets."

"The miracle had ended," Lucia concluded.

"Indeed," I said. "I was a common man again, unlucky, forsaken."

"A real man," says the psychoanalyst. "That is, a man who loses a lot and occasionally wins. I believe," Lucia says, "that you told me this episode to attempt to seduce me."

Her observation surprises me and leaves me blank. There's a silence. We're both thinking.

"You wanted me to believe," she says later, "that the problem that night was that you didn't know when to quit. But the problem is not winning or losing. Gambling wouldn't be profitable for you, as a person, even if you managed to win a lot. Your problem is not losing; it's your addiction to gambling. Telling me this episode of momentary success is an attempt to displace the conflict to an error in calculation, to a betting incontinence. That incontinence is not knowing when to quit," Lucia asserts. "The hemorrhaging incontinence is gambling."

"Sometimes you're like a strict mother," I reproach her.

"You don't need a mother," Lucia responds in a none-too-friendly voice. "Only children need mothers; you're not a child, and furthermore, you have a real mother. I have no reason to reward your apparent successes or punish your mistakes. You're the one who places yourself in a fantasy land of rewards and punishments by your persistence in gambling. If you were to win every time," she adds, "you would get bored and quit playing since, as you admit, the desire for profit is not a good reason to gamble. If you were to lose every time, you would also get bored. How many more times must you lose for this to happen? You're the one who has to establish the limit."

"Limits exist only to be exceeded," I respond.

"But when they're exceeded," Lucia refutes, "there's no more pleasure, no more joy, but only the opposite. There's no more pleasure in the tenth whiskey than in the ninth. There is malaise, loss of reality, of health, of consciousness. There is no more pleasure in the sixth straight orgasm than in the fifth. There is swelling, exhaustion, pain. The body sets the limits, in the physical as well as the mental."

"If we go on like this," I say, referring to this loathsome analysis, "you're going to make me lose the desire to gamble."

"Wasn't that your intention in coming here?"

"When a desire is extinguished, we end up naked, defenseless, impotent."

"Desire is indefatigable as long as the object changes," Lucia states.

"Is that an argument for infidelity?" I suggest, laughing. (I'm happy to have found a way to relax the tension of this dialogue.)

"I think it would be quite good if you were disloyal to the Goddess of Fortune and nurtured some other desire," the psychoanalyst responds. "But that's enough for today. We'll see you again on Friday."

No. I am not a gambler. I have never gambled. I have never entered a casino, never heard of bingo, don't know how to bet. I'm a man with no vices, no addictions, no intrigue. I pass by a slot machine indifferently. How can somebody be so hung up on such a silly game? And the bingo rooms, with their tacky decorations, their fringed chandeliers, their bright-colored uniforms (the poor doorman of Billares, required to wear a canary-colored suit and top hat like a clown). How did I withstand those countless hours of the monotonous ballad of numbers, the repeating phrases ("Gentlemen, let's begin the game. Boards sold."). Now I'm a free man. I have no dependencies, no obsessions, nor do I inject the sweet drug of luck inside purple-carpeted, silk-curtained casinos.

I have no dependencies? I depend on my job, my psychoanalyst, the order of the world. On laws, on the government, on the passage of time.

"But those are inevitable," the psychoanalyst would say.

11

The magazine's building stands in the commercial sector of the city. It is accessed through a lobby with several elevators, alarms, control panels for the private security guards, and hidden video cameras in the ceiling. Security measures must be tightened because we are receiving threats. We are often threatened by fanatics when they feel injured by an article or a photograph; and there all kinds of fanatics. There are political fanatics, religious fanatics, soccer fanatics (of a certain team, generally their own city's), rock fanatics, fashion fanatics, not to mention the psychopaths, and the members of the various mafias. There are also corporations, medical associations, lawyers' associations, architects' associations. And the traffickers: traffickers of arms, money, drugs, prostitutes, children, sex.

The threats are never executed; though more than once the building has been evacuated due to a bomb threat. The controls function very well and deter any of these fanatics or psychopaths who dare to approach the building. Once you cross the lobby, there is a large floor full of offices, conference rooms, and halls where the editing is done.

Every time I walk in I get the feeling I've entered an anthill, with its cubicles, workers, soldiers, guards, warehouses, cellars, archives, and newspaper libraries. The queen ant is the omnipotent director and principal stockholder—the portly, terribly healthy hypochondriac (only healthy people are hypochondriacs). He is pragmatic, energetic and paranoid. (Paranoiacs make excellent journalists because they are suspicious of everyone but themselves.)

I cross this room teeming with humanity and machines and I unwillingly immerse myself in my cell of the anthill. Now I'm in the anthill I guess I should buzz like everyone else.

"You have an interview at five with that actress, Liza Lancaster," the secretary tells me. "The director wants you to do it. It's an exclusive."

"Let Pedro do it," I protest. "I don't like widows, especially famous ones."

"Don't be stupid," the director's voice rebukes me over the phone. "We paid a fortune for the exclusive. Besides, she only speaks English. There's her complete file on the table."

Liza Lancaster, widow of the famous leading man. Maiden name, Sarah Kelly, born in Philadelphia, year unknown, best not to ask. She's aged astonishingly well . . . world's most beautiful eyes, high cheekbones, full, wavy hair, extremely long legs, strong personality, unruly in school, condemned to star in commercial movies, wedding with skinny, ugly, untalented actor inexplicably seductive to women.

"Impassioned marriage" (*sic*, from the magazine) brief, due to husband's premature death from cirrhosis of the liver. Burial, universal grief, Liza Lancaster dressed in black (her best color; she should always wear it, and when one funeral is over, she should quickly go to another), dubbed the "Exemplary Widow" since then by the media. Doesn't get movie contracts worthy of her after that; consequently, makes very few films. However, role as illustrious widow is tireless, eternal. She is no longer just Liza Lancaster, the strong-willed actress who rants about bad scripts and the stupid film industry, but now is Liza-Lancaster-Widow-of-Power, the skinny, half-hearted actor who drove women wild. Just published her fairly sincere, bold memoirs. Been quite successful. Hobbies: dogs and games of chance.

"You have some hobbies in common, don't you?" the director's voice interrupts over the phone. "I believe she likes animals and roulette."

"I don't have a dog and furthermore, I've quit gambling," I say.

"Not for long," he comments skeptically. "You've got an interview with this woman at five and let it be the best one of your life."

"You'll pay me extra. And I mean extra," I demand.

"One can certainly see that things have gone badly for you in the casino," he says. "Fine. So be it. By the way, tell me, what do you take for heartburn? I'm nauseous and my head aches."

"It's not heartburn," I point out. "The problem is you abuse the Vitamin C."

"How do you know it's not heartburn?"

"Because four packets of Vitamin C is too much. That's got to be the cause," I say.

"I can't stop taking Vitamin C," the director declares, agitated. "I smoked a lot when I was young, and Vitamin C lowers cholesterol."

"That still hasn't been proven," I assert. "To fight cholesterol, eat hazelnuts. One hundred grams of hazelnuts a day, preferably in the morning."

"Really?" he says enthusiastically. "I didn't know that."

"I've told you we should add a section on science to the magazine."

He only overcomes his hypochondria when it comes to business.

"Do you want me to drown? Science is too serious for a beauty-parlor magazine. The taxi's waiting to take you to the hotel. Don't even think about arriving one minute late. That woman has a bad temper."

At least she has some kind of temper.

In fact, she does have the world's most beautiful eyes. Green, with gold streaks, always moist, as if their warmth were watery and the heat of that gaze could just pour out. But that warmth contrasts with the strong lines of her face, the firmness of her bones. Her cheekbones jut out and her cheeks sink in a little; her chin has a tiny dimple in the middle, like a hint of intelligent roguishness amidst the solid expression of her face. Her forehead is broad and open; it holds up the start of a rolling, thick, iridescent head of hair and the sure weight of intelligence, excessive for an actress, a decorative object (at least according to the idiotic American industry).

"Now don't tell me you've seen all my films, because that's the worst way to start an interview," she anticipates.

She is ebullient, self-confident. She plays her role forcefully—the Exemplary Widow—but she is terribly sincere. ("I've got too few years left to waste time faking it or lying," she would say later on.) She must have extraordinary common sense. She doesn't like the world, never has liked it, but is not naive enough to presume she can change it. ("At best, one can only change one's private life a little," she says.)

"Only the good ones," I respond, trying to be flexible.

"So you've seen three," she says.

I don't tell her I've seen the other ones too.

"Everyone has to do an enormous number of foolish things to be able to do just one or two of the things that really interest them. This is true for writers, painters, reporters, actresses, film directors, and scientists. Don't try to explain it to me."

We are alone in the hotel suite. The dogs must be in another room. She travels with them, her secretary, and a couple of bodyguards. She's wearing a pretty green kimono ("the same as the color of her eyes" I will say in the magazine's detestable style), with printed designs of yellow and white bamboo. She is one of the few elegant actresses the American film industry has produced. I tell her so.

"Elegance is European, darling," she says. "We Americans have only invented canned soup. Especially crab bisque in cans, which everyone thinks is Chinese. Besides, I don't feel any particular respect for elegance," she adds. "If one doesn't have it, there's no way to get it, and if you have it, you can't lose it. That impeded my working with Fellini, my favorite director. I might have been a magnificent Lady Astor, but I never could have been a fish seller on the streets of Rome. Power was elegant too." (The first allusion to her dead husband.) "There's another mystery.

Thin, small build, pockmarks on his face, and yet the most elegant man in Hollywood. He was born in a poor neighborhood, did you know that?"

She doesn't wait for me to answer and goes on. "His entire infancy and adolescence, until he was eight years old, was spent in orphanages and the ghetto. But when a famous director, I won't tell you who, had him play a role that seemed to match his background—a delinquent born in the slums—he wasn't convincing. Without his smoking jacket, a striped shirt, and suspenders, he was not believable, even despite the fact that he spoke like a taxi driver from the Bronx."

She paused to drink from her glass of whiskey. She was drinking it slowly. She held the glass with her long fingers—so long there seemed to be more than five.

"Women loved him," she added. "I was no exception. An inexplicable, almost involuntary seduction. He wasn't charming with them (or with men); he didn't flatter them; he didn't try to make them want him. He was mean, cold, ill-humored. But he fascinated them."

"Female masochism," I interrupted.

She ignored my commentary.

"He hated movies. He considered them puerile and deceptive."

"And you?" I asked.

With a swift motion of her left hand (the one that wasn't holding the whiskey) she flipped off the tape recorder.

"I am his widow," she restated. "A role I don't like and for which I wasn't prepared. I have tried to jump out of the script, betray the script, but fiction has beaten me."

"Aristotle said fiction is more important than history," I say.

She bursts out laughing: brutal, oceanic, Pantagruelian

laughter. (The only slip of spontaneity from her studied elegance.)

"Aristotle?" she repeats. "Aristotle said that?"

I can't contain myself and I, too, start laughing.

"Aristotle," she exclaims, "I haven't heard about him since high school. I thought he was only mentioned when poor Greeks name their sons after him. You Europeans are magnificent. Cheers," she adds, "your allusion to Aristotle deserves another round," and she pours us both a drink.

When she stops laughing, the world grows dim: darkness, pain, and death return.

"Now I've resigned myself to this role. I've had worse ones in my life. Power wasn't prepared to die either. In the hospital, his body full of tubes and probes, he said, 'Liza, tell the son-of-a bitch director that this character's not right. I'm not good at dying.' "

She buried her green eyes in the liquid of her glass. They looked like two sailboats on the verge of capsizing.

"Aren't you going to ask me one of those stupid reporter questions?" she asked, emerging from her abstraction.

I felt dazzled but content, prepared to love her and improvise.

"What have you got in your bag? May I?"

Now, surprised, she just smiles.

"I'm extremely curious about women's purses," I explain. "They're like jack-in-the-boxes, magic top hats or something. You never know what you might find inside a woman's purse."

"Have you consulted a psychoanalyst about this?" Liza asked with her usual irony.

"That's not necessary," I respond. "In many languages 'bag' or 'purse' also means *sex*."

As a kid I would secretly open Michelle's purse, spread

out the contents on the rug and become ecstatic as I examined the diverse and surprising objects inside. I think she knew and sometimes put a few things in there deliberately to seduce me.

Very carefully I opened the actress's purse and reviewed its contents. I found a gold monogrammed cigarette case, a designer lighter, a gold pen, a glass case with a tiny sea horse ("For luck," she said), and a splendid, oval, extremely valuable mother-of-pearl chip from the casino at Monte Carlo. The piece was quite soft to the touch; my fingers slid over it again and again, enamored. I extracted it from Liza Lancaster's purse and caressed it without a word. She understood the gesture and said:

"I'm a gambler. After fifty, my friend, sex ceases to be of interest; an exhausting acrobatics. At that point, one understands that it was not strictly in one's head, as the psychologists would have us believe, but in one's hormones and ovaries. My hormones have simmered down and my ovaries are old. When sex becomes boring, you have to discover another emotion, another vice. I like gambling. Sometimes I think it's the only thing that keeps me alive. Besides I have sadistic tendencies: I usually win. Power always lost. You may find that surprising since he was a shrewd person, but he became extraordinarily vulnerable when he gambled. He believed luck was masculine. Power was sadistic with women, but not with men."

"You, however, are sadistic with anyone," I ventured ironically.

"I'm very traditional, my dear," she answered. "For me, luck is female and I have never faltered before any woman.

"Power lost because he was a man who didn't know his limits," Liza Lancaster added. Very seriously she said: "For him, gambling was metaphysical, do you understand?"

66

"Yes," I said softly.

"How absurd!" she remarked, tossing her gorgeous hair. "I don't understand that hang-up at all. I'm a practical woman. I have never felt it, but I loved him for it. When I met him, he had already begun the game."

"What game?" I ask just to keep her talking. I'm under the spell of her slightly hoarse voice, her dark hair, her long legs.

"The game he'd initiated with limits. A private game, with no witnesses, as you can understand. You could accompany him for one round, stand next to him for a while, but in the most profound challenge, he was alone, even knowing he would lose. It's like throwing blind dice without numbers. There was no chance of winning, not one; and he still bet. To ignorant people, that was senseless, crazy. But I loved him for that kind of heroism. He was the same about drinking; he didn't quit even with the cirrhosis. A suicidal pride, if you must, but he made it grandiose."

The night was falling like a shroud . . . simply that. The night was covering us with its lapidary darkness. It fit the melancholy that goes along with the death of a hero, the melancholy of a fortuitous encounter never to be repeated.

"I win because I bet small," she continued. "A quiet old age, with my dogs, my bodyguards, and my house in New York. Poker with friends and a few visits to the casino. This is achievable. But Power's desire was impossible and that's why he wanted it so much. True desires can't be named. They are scandalous and provoke God's ire. As for you and your magazine," she subtly changed her tone of voice and stood up, "you can invent the kind of conventional interview people like. Talk about my dogs, my house in New York, my loneliness as an inconsolable widow or whatever. My secretary will give you a complete file. It's been a pleasure meeting you," she said and extended her hand, "but I'm a little tired."

The end had been as abrupt as the beginning.

Reluctantly I walked toward the door.

Then she motioned me to stop and, looking me in the eyes, she said, "I know desires can be changed. Power couldn't, or didn't want to. In the end, he was nothing but a boy who'd been mistreated in his childhood and, to compensate, he aspired to be God. After fifty, we all become philosophers. It must be genetic, something to do with preserving the species. Maybe I got that pearl chip you were so fond of only because I didn't want it that much. My lucky number is twenty-seven. What's yours?"

"I still haven't found it," I said, half-smiling.

"Don't be stubborn," she advised. "Sometimes I think I win at gambling because I can't win at anything else."

When I left the interview, I needed a woman violently. But is wasn't just for sex. (In reality, nothing is easier for a man—as long as he's not alone on an island—than getting sex. It's offered for a thousand pesetas on any corner, for a little more it can be bought in comfortable hotels, fancy cafés, hygienic saunas, aseptic massage parlors; you can order it by phone, messenger, mail, or TV.) But this was something else. I didn't want just to touch a woman and have her touch me, I didn't want to take in a strange body, then leave. I realized that my conversation with Liza Lancaster had provoked nostalgia of a woman. Nostalgia is always a masked disguise. It was a violent need, and hard to satisfy at that moment. Then, without meaning to, without expecting to, I thought of Claudia.

"There is no desire without a symbol," Lucia had said a week before.

And now, unintentionally, I evoked Claudia.

I didn't evoke the Claudia of our amorous quarrels, our disappointments, but the one I was looking for and never found; a woman with Claudia's body, Claudia's breasts, Claudia's legs, and her slow, embracing orgasms; but what I called *Claudia* wasn't the Claudia I'd loved.

It had been a while since we'd known anything about each other. "I want to break up with you," she said, and I took it literally. She wanted to *break me up*. Maybe I wanted to break her too. We broke each other and ever since, silence separated us. We had survived, true, but neither one of us could understand how.

"Every time I lose, in bingo or at the casino," I had told the psychoanalyst last week, "I blame it on Claudia. Claudia's the one who brought me bad luck. I was thinking about her when I picked the wrong number and lost the game."

"What game did you lose with her?" Lucia asked with irony.

"I don't know," I answer. "We were playing something very important between us; a raising of the ante, a challenge."

"Are you sure she won?" she asks.

" 'Cover me' Claudia sometimes said when we made love. 'You are biblical, señora,' I would answer. When I'm gambling, I wonder if 'covering' the seventeen or the fifteen is a way of continuing to cover her."

"She's not asking you anymore," the psychoanalyst responds sharply. "You haven't answered whether or not you believe she won."

"I don't know what we were playing, what the prize was, which was the losing round, so I can't know if anybody won."

"Nobody plays blindly," Lucia says. "As a gambling man, you should know that."

"Maybe I'm so much a gambler that I undertook the most important gamble of my life, against her; a blind game, not knowing the prize or what I could lose."

Now, after the interview with Liza Lancaster, this violent need for a woman again carries me unconsciously toward Claudia. I'd like to call her, as if nothing had happened, as if I hadn't been broken, as if she hadn't been broken; and removing all the resentment, all the envy, all the bitterness, we find ourselves in a deep, cool embrace, and I tell her about my interview with Liza Lancaster, protect her, let her protect me. But it's an impossible fantasy. it's not just Claudia who wouldn't be able to overcome this long period of silence, resentment, bitterness; I couldn't either.

"I suspect you believe that despite appearances, Claudia was the one who lost. That's why, out of some obscure guilt, you punish yourself by betting at the gambling tables, where you can lose. In this way, you relieve your feeling of guilt," Lucia interpreted.

I squirmed nervously in my seat.

" 'You and I are incompatible,' Claudia told me at the end. I thought it was a line from a bad novel."

"One has to end some way," Lucia defends her. "She gave you a good option: a tie. But maybe you didn't want a tie. You wanted, as always, to defeat or die."

Hence, this violent need for a woman cannot be satisfied in Claudia.

Meanwhile, the night has taken over the city, with its display case of unfulfilled desires: golden lights on the buildings (what parties, what splendor I don't know), flashy cars in show windows, exclusive gems in velvet cases, neon signs evoking faraway lands . . . Bali . . . Manhattan . . . Milan . . . Venice.

If I can't touch or talk to Claudia, I'd like to touch or talk the psychoanalyst. I detest the moments when I want a woman so urgently. Resolved, I head for a phone booth. The long audible silence that separates me from Claudia (a silence of screams, reproaches, jealousy, misunderstandings) doesn't stop me, however, from talking to Lucia. On the contrary, I pay her to listen to me. I dial her home number, not the office. (She gives it out to her patients in case of an emergency.) After a couple of rings, I hear: "I can't answer your call right now. If you'd like to leave a message, you have two minutes to speak after the tone. Thank you."

"It's Jorge," I say to the machine. "Actually, I'd like to have an extra session, but not in the office. In a hotel. In an expensive hotel with a big bed and cotton sheets, champagne and oysters for breakfast. Afterward, if you wish, we can go back to this game of analysis, with paid visits, forty-five minutes and all that."

I didn't say anything else because my time had run out.

I went into an open bar, drank a beer, and headed for the slot machine. This one had the jingle "Tea for Two." How ironic. Maybe that's why I won: three beautiful *cirsas*, that looked like gold. The coins began to fall without the slightest effort.

"You want company?" a young girl with a comb in her hair like a Cherokee Indian asked me. The machine was still spewing coins. They always end with a trio of red cherries: the Holy Trinity. I imagined the Cherokee harnessed to a horse or something like that.

I have never been able to console myself of the absence

71

of one woman by the presence of another woman.

I thought about Liza, I thought about Claudia, I thought about Lucia. None of these three was right for me at that moment.

"I don't need company," I told the Cherokee wearing black boots covered with silver-plated doodads. "But I'll buy you a beer."

"Thanks, pal," she said.

Everyone disguises himself as best he can.

12

'm fed up," I tell the psychoanalyst in late July. "I'm going to the country."

Usually in August, I hole up in my apartment, surrounded by milk bottles, cigarette boxes, unread books, aspirin, a fan, and bags of oranges. I live like a bat. I only go out at night to roam the deserted city which looks like the aftermath of a bomb explosion: a heat bomb.

"That seems like a good idea," Lucia remarks.

She probably thinks it's a good idea because she wants to take a vacation too. To forget, for one month, all these nuts who come to make confession to her as if she were the Universal Mother, the Great Teacher, the Mother Superior.

"Where will you go?" I ask, acting nonchalant.

"That's my business," she answers laconically.

That doesn't seem fair. I've already told her I'll be going to Michelle's house.

"We'll see each other again when you return," Lucia

specifies. "You'll tell me what you've done, how you've been feeling. It'll be good for you to relax a little."

I feel like a sick person who's been prescribed fresh air, swimming, berry-picking, and horseback riding. I pay too much for a prescription like that.

"Shall I bring you a quartered rabbit as a souvenir, or a sprig of basil?" I ask sarcastically.

"Instead of bringing me something, it would be better for you to give up a few things," Lucia says severely. I lay it out on the table.

"The psychoanalytic relationship," I tell her, "is a sadomasochistic drama with interchangeable roles."

"I think that analysis can be applied to just about anything," Lucia does not refute me.

I'm starting to feel frustrated. Whenever I start to feel like this I end up in the bingo parlor or casino.

"You can send me a postcard if you want," Lucia volunteers from the doorway as I'm leaving.

Is she afraid I won't come back? Does she hope the postcard—saying what, I don't know—will serve as a link between this last session and the next one, after a month? Or did she propose it to console me?

"I don't send postcards," I lie, and it seems a timid revenge.

13

I like talking about numbers; I like seeing them jump, verifying their frequency, pursuing their absence, loving or hating them.

THE SEX OF NUMBERS

Number 1 is a shy man with a small dick; number 2, a sophisticated French whore; number 3, a fat little eunuch who sings opera; number 6, a pregnant woman; number 9, an old working woman with a hunched back; number 11, a gay couple; 21, mother and child; 22, a lesbian couple; 61, the missionary position; 69, as everybody knows, simultaneous oral sex; 77, two old faggots; 80, a senile married couple.

When I was small my mother used to carry a little mirror in her purse. This mirror had numbers inscribed on the back, one through a hundred, as well as a brief description of their meanings in dreams, according to old, popular tradition. I loved reading them. Seventeen was a feathered serpent; 8 was a snake; 7 was a chicken; 11, teeth; 6 meant a lot of money, and 99, poverty.

"They're superstitions," my mother told me condescendingly. (Michelle has always been a highly rational woman.)

I liked it when the numbers were ominous or symbolic animals. They were alive.

I returned to *Chez Michelle* in the summer, as I did every year. As we ate dinner—her Stroganoff was superb—I asked her about the mirror.

"What mirror?" she said.

"Your pocket mirror. The one with the numbers on the back," I answered.

Michelle laughed. "You and your things," she said. "I'm sure it's lost. It was a silly mirror. I got it from one of the stores as a giveaway."

It's strange because Michelle is a woman who keeps things, like most French women. It's hard for her to part with anything. War mentality or something like that.

Claudia thought it very strange that I called my mother Michelle; never called her "mom," or "mother." But I like it better this way. Michelle. She thinks it's natural; her role of woman over that of mother.

Every summer I go to her house/restaurant situated in an old town in Ampurdán and I say: "Michelle, I'm coming to your house."

"Her house is not yours also?" Claudia asked me.

No. It's Michelle's house, and I like it that way. Her house with its big basket of old brown straw hanging from the rusty iron balcony and the homemade flower decorations with dried stalks in those quaint clay pots. Give Michelle some old junk, a few weeds and an old stove, and she'll cook up a delicious meal with it, or she'll transform a few gloomy rooms into luxury accommodations. I admire women for their ability to create.

"Nor is my apartment Michelle's," I told Claudia. "When she comes to visit, she tells me in advance. There is no concupiscence between us," I concluded.

I was sulking a little because Michelle didn't know where that mirror with the imprinted numbers was.

Later, Michelle served flaming banana crêpes with honey.

14

The town, with its remarkably well-conserved medieval center, situated amidst ample wheat fields and luscious orchards, is about a hundred and fifty kilometers from the city. However, its ancient look, slow pace and the obstinacy of its habits make it seem quite foreign, distant, in both time and space, as if you were separated from the city by some insurmountable barrier. When you drive there, you enter gradually, as if every tree, every patch of grass, were a zone in limbo which, once passed, is a step closer to paradise.

It's a very quiet place, though during the summer, the tourists upset the peace and harmony of the old stone paths and the ancient farms where the sheep graze. That summer it was very hot. All day long the cicadas kept up an incessant racket, and during the night, the teenagers from the city matched that with the deafening racket from their motorcycles.

The first afternoon, I saw a young boy with copper-colored skin and black eyes, clearly a foreigner, furtively prowling around outside Michelle's house. He had a soft, gentle, utterly seductive smile. His dazzling white teeth shone against his dark complexion. As always, Michelle didn't say a word about him. We were both reserved as far as our personal relationships go. I assumed he was a rural worker; one of the many who come up from North Africa for the harvest and who find it difficult to survive on their own in a strange town.

He was wandering around Michelle's house about the time when the locals were just getting up from their naps and the dense, sweet aroma of roast lamb impregnated the fields.

Tired of circling Michelle's still closed restaurant in vain, the boy stealthily crept to the town's only bar situated in the tree-lined plaza with the stone fountain and dry riverbed. In front of the bar were a few white iron tables with open umbrellas advertising some brand of vermouth, the spot where the town's old people usually gather to entertain themselves with boisterous card games.

In the bar beneath a high-arched ceiling is a pool table lit by one small light bulb covered with a brass shade. It's a decent pool table, for a small town bar. The cues are new, the felt of the runner is barely used, and the sides are studded with metal. I challenged the boy to a game. I never once told him I was Michelle's son. He accepted right away, in need of a little sociability.

I carefully arranged the black rack and placed the white ball in the worn circle. I'd won the draw, so I had to start. I aimed the smooth yellow surface at the vertex of the triangle formed by the other balls. The shot went off, swift and precise, like a bullet. I listened to the dry knock of the balls as they scattered. I sank two in a single shot: stripes.

I shot again and this time I put the six ball in one of the pockets. He watched my movements with apparent disinterest, prepared to lose. I sank another. On my next shot, I deliberately faltered to give him a chance. He played well and I couldn't regain the advantage I had. As I applied the blue chalk to the tip of my cue in preparation to sink the eight ball, I wondered how many things this foreigner was prepared to lose in the hope of winning just one, the loving protection of Michelle.

I aimed precisely, taking my time, and the shiny ball shot into the right pocket.

"You know the difference between a good player and a bad one?" I asked the boy, who had humbly accepted his defeat. He shook his head diffidently.

"A good player is always prepared to lose before he wins."

15

On a piece of walnut bark, in her big oval arabesque handwriting, Michelle wrote *Obert* (Catalan for open); she drew a lily on both sides of the word and hung the sign from the balcony. Over the thick wood door, inside a small glass-covered niche, she placed the menu, handwritten on parchment in red letters. *Chez Michelle.* A pleasant, rustic stone dining room, a vase of wild flowers, classical music, and a waitress—also French—who served a limited but exquisite fare.

I don't think Michelle's found much difference between Aix, where she was born, and this town constructed on rocks in lower Ampurdán where she has lived for all these years. But in Aix, I remember, there were more fields of lavender. Here, her restaurant/house is surrounded by sunflowers that bow their heads in the afternoon. My infancy? The warm smell of sunflower pie, the residue from the oil (a smell I sometimes search in vain for in the city, which

smells only of gasoline and old musty laundry combined).
Nor must she have found much difference between the
French spoken in Aix and the ancient *langue d'oc* spoken
in this Ampurdán village, though its harshness contrasts
slightly with the superficial friendliness of French.

When I come to visit—once a year in the summer—I like
to go with her to the market in the next town over. We get
up early, Michelle grabs the bags, and we climb into her old
black Peugeot ("the dinosaur"), adorned with two yellow
flags on the bumpers. We cross the smooth stone bridge
over the nonexistent river and the path of tall poplars whose
leaves sway gently in the wind. Michelle loves the land, the
smell of lamb, the shifting skies, the dripping of hidden
water between the stones. She knows the different kinds of
lettuce, peppers, and bananas. At the market she argues
with the farmers on an equal footing, buys the best potatoes
and the most tender onions. I, an urban animal accustomed
to cement and streetlights, hang back a little, observing her
like the prince consort. Between the dried garlic and the
pungent smell of ripe peaches, I feel like I'm briefly con-
senting to a lost paradise, the paradise of childhood, which
is only a paradise as long as we are free to come and go as
we please. While she shops, Michelle, ecstatic, pictur-
esquely ecstatic before a bundle of mauve-colored penny-
royals or a cluster of translucent golden grapes, ignores me
completely.

La Mere Michelle, a good French woman, is extraordinarily thrifty, without being stingy. She won't skimp on
condiments, but she won't be swindled either. We never
speak of money. We consider it a vulgar subject. Not
money, not women, and not men. Not once has she confided
a thing to me about those young foreigners who, one summer after another, circle the restaurant like cats in heat.

82

Over the years, Michelle's visits to the city have decreased. She cannot stand the noise, the crowds, the pollution, the hostility. She prefers that I visit her, in August, and at least once during the winter. She bought this farm when I was small, when she decided to pick up and move to the country. It has several rooms and I can stay in any one of them. I appreciate the fact that she hasn't reserved one for me. I would take that as a hidden reproach, an accusation of abandonment.

The only trips she takes (in her old Peugeot, the dinosaur) are to Paris; but only rarely. For my part, I'm not the least drawn to Paris. I prefer the South American jungles, where my father probably disappeared. Michelle is quiet. The subject of my father annoys her. I like people who get irritated easily without even trying to understand, without even trying to establish some kind of justice.

"An absent and idealized father," the psychoanalyst said one day. "In spite of your mother's irritation."

"I didn't miss him consciously," I answered. Michelle was both mother and father at the same time: affection and law in the same person. She avoids conflict. I only started thinking about him when I chose his profession—journalism—and I supposed he'd disappeared into the jungle chasing after a lost revolution or some Indian squaw with nice hips. Another lost cause: desire.

At night, the cistern of *Chez Michelle* sounds like the siren of a stranded boat.

16

The room in *Chez Michelle* where I sleep has a stone floor, white walls, and a slanted ceiling held up by thick hardwood rafters. Extraordinarily austere, like a monk's quarters, the room has just one low bed covered with a scrap quilt, sewn by Michelle, a large wooden chest with steel bolts, and a ceramic washstand. Without wanting to, as I get up in the morning, I find my reflection in the oval mirror above the washstand. I look at myself: a strange fellow with urban bags under his eyes, nicotine-stained teeth, born in Aix—who cares—whose lungs, full of carbon monoxide, receive the blessing of fresh air for a few days.

I spend the first two days of vacation at *Chez Michelle* just lying about, numb and drowsy from an excess of oxygen. To regain myself, I would have to plunge into a gambling hall full of smoke. The town is like one of those radical priests who start their reformation by making us feel worse.

17

The only game Michelle plays regularly is the newspaper crossword puzzle. Every morning—Michelle is an early riser—she climbs into her Peugeot and drives down to *La Bisbal* to buy the paper. Under the ancient arches of the once Roman city, the melancholy stores open: a barber shop with old swivel chairs with metal pedals, a bakery with sponge cakes and almond dough cookies, a dime store displaying cotton long underwear in the window, an old café with a modernist canopy and its table and chairs hiding beneath the shade of the illustrious arches, and a kiosk with newspapers and magazines. Michelle buys the paper, opens to the crossword section, orders *café con leche,* and shortly thereafter has finished the puzzle. Ever since I can remember she has kept this routine, like one small, satisfying vice. She practices it every day, winter and summer. But in the winter, the old café doesn't set out the tables and chairs under the arches, so Michelle sits inside, under the crafted ceiling facing the laminated mirrors. She has always done this, even when the sight of a woman alone in a café was cause for suspicion.

She never leaves the crossword puzzle unfinished. It's a challenge. But Michelle was always a liberal and self-confident woman. The pages of the paper interest her less and less. 5: ". . . as you would have others do unto you," Jesus said.

—DO UNTO OTHERS. Michelle displays a chill reserve toward the world, which betrays a deep irritation. The world didn't ask her opinion when it was organizing itself, so she can't help but respond with utter disregard. 12: "Another name for cowboy movies"—WESTERNS. I think solving crossword puzzles is like a test of self-sufficiency; the only mental test she'll subject herself to . . . with no one's intervention, because Michelle has always been independent, free, autonomous. True, she fought some battles: a political committee, a feminist liberation movement. But she usually doesn't talk about that, the same as she doesn't talk about my father's absence. 8: "Chemicals used on film"—EMULSION.

Sometimes I bring her a few copies of my magazine. She leafs through them, but has nothing to say about them. I can read some of her thoughts.

The afternoon I arrived, I was in the town bar having a beer like one more tourist (no one had recognized me yet) and I suddenly saw Michelle walk by with her straw bag on her way to the fields where she likes to pick berries. Erect, elegant, blond, wrapped in a black shawl with yellow frets, exposing her beautiful sun-bronzed shoulders, she attracted the stare of the regulars. It was hot, they were bored, but they commented out loud, unaware of my presence.

86

"She's something, that Michelle."

"Really something, yup."

15: "Thirteen coins given at weddings as a symbolic price of bride"—*ARRAS*.

"Are you attracted to your mother?" Lucia asked me at the beginning of my therapy.

"She's something, that Michelle," I confessed.

18

My father was born here near these colonnades. He emigrated to Aix with his family after the war. One summer—Michelle says it was summer—he met my mother and in a month they were married. The marriage didn't last long (Michelle thinks love and marriage are incompatible), and one day, unaware that I had already been conceived ("condoms weren't that safe in those days," Michelle says), he disappeared from Aix, headed for the South American jungle. He wanted to start a newspaper, win a war, write a book. Apparently Michelle never forgave him. And yet, shortly after I was born, we moved to this town so reminiscent of Aix, with its wheat fields, sheep roaming the stone paths, and sunflowers that substitute for lavender.

There is an enigma, a mystery about premature deaths and disappearances. My father vanished, so my nostalgia is an illusion, because I didn't know him. Michelle's resentment, on the other hand, is ambivalent. She hates him for abandoning her, but believes that had she been a man, she would have done the same thing.

19

Once a year, in late August, on those hot nights laden with the sweet aroma of roast lamb, Michelle organizes a poker game on the farm. She invites the deputy mayor (a robust, hook-nosed truck driver with weather-beaten skin), the French psychiatrist (a skinny, bald man with thick glasses who summers in the town), and the owner of the bar in the plaza.

At that hour the doors of the small restaurant have already closed. In that one annual game, they play until dawn. "The psychiatrist doesn't like to lose," Michelle remarks, amazed. She believes psychiatrists, like God, should be imperturbable.

I don't participate. I don't like to play with people I know. I'm a sensitive player. Emotions—sympathy, compassion—disturb me, make me vulnerable, fragile.

"A gambler shouldn't have feelings," Michelle says.

Michelle plays *against* others; I only play *against* luck.

Antich, the best chess player in college, used to winning up to fifteen games consecutively, was unable, however, to beat Clara, an attractive classmate. At that point, Antich realized he was in love with her.

"I don't like your poker face," I told the psychoanalyst during one of the first sessions. Lucia is a beautiful woman, very attractive, but she was listening to me with a cold, fixed expression.

"Exactly," she said. "A psychoanalyst must wear a poker face."

In Michelle's town, there are no casinos, no bingo parlors, no game rooms. Just pool in the bar and a few decks of cards for tedious summer games. The farmers don't bet. To them, money is sacred. Luck, the crazy wheel of fortune, belongs to fantasy, ambition, the frustrated desires of big cities. Rural games are much more primitive. They don't involve money; only concrete, tangible goods: a pig, a cow, a chicken, a mule, or personal values revered by the community like courage, strength, or cunning. Running bulls, rock throwing, hunting rabbits, climbing a ridge, making a human castle are ritual, collective games, and those who play them may lose their lives, but not money, the way city people do in their gambling parlors. And if the urbanite wins, he only wins money, that is he wins the means, not the end. (The soldiers who bet on Jesus' tunic at the door of the tomb were urbanites, as were the Spaniards who bet on the great Aztec Temple of the Sun in old Mexico: a captain and a corporal.)

My summer stays in the town are brief. While at first I feel fortified by the pure air, the dry smell of hay, the sweet perfume of honeysuckle, the night jasmine, soon I start to feel anxious. Michelle, who perceives my restlessness, remarks between her teeth: "You work so hard that you don't even know how to fill the time when you have a few free days."

And yet, there's something I admire about rural customs: the absence of everything superfluous. Objects have no socially representative value; they're there because they *function,* because they're useful (the shovel, the pitchfork, the washstand, the big chest, the clay pots) and the incidental, the banal does not exist. The "adornments," rustic and primitive like straw baskets or glazed vases, lack sophistication, they're made of basic materials, extracted from the earth. Objects, tools, last longer than any lifetime, and if they break, they're quickly repaired.

The townspeople don't eat at Michelle's restaurant. It's the urbanites who come (after reserving tables by phone) to Michelle's restaurant (listed in the main tourist guides).

"I haven't seen your neighbor, the stable owner," I tell Michelle. (An absence in the town is striking. Since everything has its place and time, it does not go unnoticed.)

"She moved," Michelle answers curtly, the way she does when she doesn't want to talk about something.

How strange. She was born in this town, married here, had her children here, became a widow here, just like the ten generations before her.

"Her son died," Michelle explains. "She refused to go on living in the same house, the same town, full of memories. She moved twenty kilometers away, to her cousin's house.

Twenty kilometers is a long way for someone who's always lived in the same place, the home of her ancestors, her memories. Like an exile. Like crossing an ocean and mountains. The exile of my father. Between Aix and Barcelona, there's a lot more than twenty kilometers.

In the city, where it's almost impossible to get an apartment, no one moves when their son or husband or cat dies.

I dedicate an entire day to observing the events of the town: a journalistic assignment as they say. ("Change of environment," the psychoanalyst advised. Cheap advice for such a high price.)

Taking refuge on the terrace of *Chez Michelle,* armed with a telescope she gave me a couple of years ago, paper, and a pen, I make up the imaginary pages of a rural newspaper.

4:15—A herd of sheep arrives. Its color mixes with the color of the freshly cut hay. They meander with bowed heads and gather together in groups. Two of them stand out from the rest; black ones. A bushy white dog guards them along with a middle-aged woman holding a staff. I wonder if this woman has ever seen the city.

4:30—A dragonfly with translucent wings starts flying around my head.

5:00—I discover some newly potted plants on the terrace that Michelle bought at the market yesterday. They keep the mosquitoes away.

On the tenth tile, sixth row, counting from the right, there's a swallow's nest.

A beautiful, honey-colored cat furtively climbs the wall covered with honeysuckle and bougainvillea. When it reaches the top, it hunches up, stalking. I don't know what it's watching, but it's tense, alert, on the verge of pouncing.

6:10—Weather conditions: watertight calm of the afternoon is interrupted by a swirling cool breeze. It comes from the ocean.

6:15—A hummingbird races by with a twig in its beak that's longer than its whole body. *Damn.* With this sudden wind, the nest is bound to fall apart. It will have to be fixed.

The church bells chime on the hour, the quarter hour, and the half hour. Michelle does not go to church. She's a liberal, a free-thinker, an atheist and feminist, normal for a woman who was still young in the seventies.

With the telescope I make out the poisonous berries of the hedges. You know they're poisonous by their beauty. Like mushrooms and like some women.

I don't know the names of the majority of trees and plants around here, nor do I recognize most of the insects and birds. Labeling nature must have been the work of the poets. I am an urbanite, I only comprehend men and women. Someone had to distinguish the walnut from the oak, try their fruit, classify them. Someone discovered the metaphor of weeping and the willow; someone named the blue stalks of the bilberries, tried the green berries (indigestible) and the ripe ones ("And saw that they were good"), separated the almonds, distilled the poppies, dried the sunflower seeds, and baked the mud to make bricks.

I wonder if the invention of numbers was more important than roasting meat.

7:00—The sweet, thick smell of roast lamb wafts up, as it does every night.

Every year in late August, looking at this dark country sky you can witness a cascade of shooting stars. They flash for an instant, trace a golden arc, then vanish. Last night I saw four. ("Six," Michelle corrects, who has a wider radius of observation.)

The magazine's double summer edition is dedicated to celebrities' vacations. Parties on cruises across the Mediterranean, rock concerts, all-night clubs, international adulterous affairs. A grand exposé of human flesh: tits in the open

94

air, asses covered by tiny silk triangles, shining biceps, tan legs, tattoos. And affairs. Publicity stunt affairs, extraordinary affairs, noble affairs, cinematographic affairs, banking affairs, theatrical affairs, juvenile affairs, menopausal affairs, political affairs, vulgar affairs, and exotic affairs. Affairs and break-ups. A survey conducted by the magazine reveals that black-lace affairs with red and white trim are back in style. The public declaration of a marquis, renowned flirt: "I never go to bed with a woman whose lingerie costs under five thousand pesetas."

The magazine's circulation goes up in the summer.

"People want easy literature," the director says. I wonder where he gets the word "literature." He usually talks about "product."

Along with the summer edition, we give away a little packet of suntan lotion.

In the morning, in the town, I solve the chess puzzle in Michelle's paper. Queen's Knight-six to King's Bishop-four. I solve it in ten seconds, a good player's time. I'm in shape.

I wake up early. Time here is different from time in the city. I go to bed early too. A pleasant drowsiness invades me after dinner as I watch the shooting stars and I rest calmly, pleasurably, until the next day. In my apartment in the city, I often suffer from insomnia. When the game rooms close, I get nervous and excited (after having lost, which is what usually happens), and I look for an open bar to get a drink. But that doesn't calm me down either. I know all the night owls—men and women. People who've lost all interest in work or sex (disillusioned lawyers, unemployed actresses, alcoholic reporters, informants, jobless movie directors, bankrupt gamblers, coke addicts, unpublished writers, prostitutes, divorced men and women, models, broke speculators). They're putting off that fateful moment when they

have to return to an empty apartment or a hostile room-
mate. They consume everything they can get their hands
on: alcohol, cigarettes, marijuana, hash, coke, pistachios,
French fries, and juices, with an uneasiness that betrays
their inner turmoil.

After losing, when I get home, I promise myself to
change my life. I'll eat yogurt, smoke light cigarettes, and
I will not set another foot inside a casino. I'll take valerian
instead of sleeping pills, I'll open a savings account, join a
gym, and ask for a raise. All I'll have to do then is contract
a girlfriend, get married, and have kids. But this perspective
leaves me so listless and desolate, I fall asleep—after ingest-
ing a Valium—with a silent entreaty: "Oh God, save me
from mediocrity."

But at *Chez Michelle* I go to bed before midnight and
wake up early.

Now, after a week, I begin to wonder what I've lost.

It's enough to prick your foot with a thistle, contract nasal
allergies from the hay, throw up from an unripe berry, get
fleas in a stable, be bitten by a savage dog, or verify that the
shutters in all the houses move when you walk through
town, for the bucolic life imagined by the vacationing urbanite to reveal its hostility.

20

he last night of my stay in the town, Michelle had a lot of customers: urbanites on vacation just in from the city. They're charmed by the stone house with its rustic, unvarnished tables, old wine bottles used as candleholders, and its dried flower arrangements.

In the winter, Michelle opens the restaurant only on weekends. During the long, wet, windy season, she entertains herself by weaving small baskets. It gets dark earlier: Michelle lights the pine logs in the fireplace and sometimes roasts a couple of onions or a slab of meat over the embers. She listens to music (the melancholy *lieder* of Schumann, or the last works of Strauss) and she reads. Basically, Michelle reads books about animals. She says that had she not met my father when she did, she definitely would have gone to Africa to study the habits of gorillas, lions, and chimpanzees. That's why I've brought her a very special present: a book by Subiros, a Catalan anthropologist, who argues that gorillas and many monkey species display cultural behaviors not based on instinct.

Sometimes she gets visits from old friends from the "make love not war" era. "I like testing them," Michelle admits. "I talk to them about the language of whales, the cultural activities of chimps, and the feelings of loneliness experienced by elephants. The most narcissistic," she explains, "can't stand the subject and try to change it. They like to think it's an obsession that's come over me with old age. Others question the research. The bad ones interpret my interest and curiosity in animals as a displacement of the libido. They attribute it to the absence of your father. They don't know that I was more interested in gorillas before I met that young rebel, the selfish dreamer who went off to America to start a paper, win a war or fuck natives."

"What book did my father want to write?"

"Any book; his own novel," Michelle says after the customers have left.

No two novels are alike. And for some, there are no novels at all, just TV.

"I'd like you to stay a few more days," Michelle says that night.

No, Michelle, there's no returning. You can't ever go back. Ever. Ulysses doesn't return. His son, friends, neighbors do not recognize him. He doesn't go back to Ithaca. He goes to a place where they no longer recognize him. That might be exactly why my father never came back—he knew returning was impossible. Michelle had become someone else (he left a newlywed bride who had become a mother), and a stranger—I, slobbering, terrified, dependent like all kids, selfish, sadistic, dominating, like all kids—inhabited the house and the desire. If he hadn't already written the book—something we would never know—his return could have been another book.

But in order for me to go, to abandon you again (I am a lover who comes and goes, Michelle), painlessly, I have to experience some desire. Something has to drive me, lead me to the city quickly, to my apartment, to the editorial office, to work. Only desire—albeit illusory—saves us from the melancholy of loss, from the melancholy of passings, from the melancholy of impermanence.

And the desire I have, the only desire I have—I will never confess to you—is to gamble again. My home is not my white, pristine apartment, nor is it the magazine's feverish editorial office with its humming computers and busy watchmen, its fax that vomits kilometers of paper. My home, Michelle, my home is the casino with its warm chandeliers, the red moquette that lines the halls, the luxurious washrooms with their many doors, its large marble tables, the parallel mirrors, the doormen who recognize me and greet me with a slight bow of the head.

"How are you, sir?" they ask me. "Would you like something to drink?"

There I feel welcome, comfortable, cozy. I choose a table, try to pick an empty one, buy three boards, look at the screen, light a cigarette, sit back in the chair, grab a pen, and, like a sweet indulgence, like a meaningless song, I start to listen to the dripping of numbers, the arbitrary combination of figures.

say good-bye to Michelle, to vacation, climb into the white Escort with its sunroof ("You can contemplate the moon, the stars," the salesman told me and I laughed. Who cares about contemplating the moon and stars in the city? Where can you see them? But the argument, so ingenuous and childlike, seemed nice, so I bought it), and I shoot out toward the highway, heading for the city. I like fast cars and women with slow orgasms. I look at the illuminated clock on the dashboard: two hours until Billares opens. A hundred and fifty kilometers. I'll arrive by the eleventh or twelfth game. In the fastest bingo parlors, there's a game every eight or nine minutes.

"Detox," the psychoanalyst advised. "Break your habits. Just as you got used to gambling, you can get used to living without gambling. But first you need a change of environment."

A hundred and fifty kilometers: long enough to think, to

decide whether or not I should gamble again. I can spend the first fifty kilometers, for example—full of trees: cedar, pine, poplar, willows, carob trees—resisting the temptation to play. The repetitive refrain of the slot machines ("The Third Man," "Domino," "Dream of Love") and its infantile seduction. The Pavlovian reflex, or something like that. But it's not the sound that attracts me. I'm much more drawn by the lights of the slots, the colors that blink on and off, the series of electronic figures on the screen—apples, pears, strawberries, grapes, bells.

"A patently infantile solicitation," Lucia observes.

"I'm not one of those adults who delights in the death of the child I once was," I quickly answered. "I don't fancy the idea of being a child all the time," I added. "Only once in a while, for fun."

For fifty kilometers—it begins to drizzle lightly, a late summer rain. The steam rises from the trees, the bluish color of the mountains, the smell of the wet earth—I can disparage the electronic figures of that childish tombolo, the old repetitive jingles, the yellowish-green uniforms of the doorman at Billares, the excessive makeup of the girls who work there, the coarseness of the clients. Those stupid machines with the crude drawings and colored little stars, the garish decor of the bingo parlors to impress country bumpkins who confuse ostentation with luxury, the way they confuse journalism with literature, government with the state, order with repression, and eroticism with pornography.

But then, if I resist my desire to gamble, the world seems less meaningful. The light-falling drizzle seems dirty, meager, stingy; the trees along the road, rickety, barren; the highway, a path for feverish ants; the city, a buried Babel, moldy, full of gas and noise; the editorial office, a chaotic

101

brothel; love, an exchange of secretions.

If I don't gamble, I have a hundred kilometers of hundred-year-old trees left, the skeleton of the cement factories that look like tattered brontosauruses, the slot machines at the toll booths, the hot narrow apartment (a well-decorated cell), the magazine's asses and tits, a book of Steiner's essays on the bedside table, or how about one of those American movies with the psychopath of the hour making a suit out of swatches of skin from his victims?

No. I don't want to be a man who doesn't gamble, the kind who's overcome the vice and accepts his limitations. I don't want to be a man who doesn't gamble so that he doesn't lose. I don't want to become a forty-year-old, losing his hair, getting fat, playing tennis on weekends, humbling himself before his superiors, tyrannizing his subordinates, and feeling attracted to fifteen-year-old adolescents. (Voluntary losers possess a certain grandiosity about them. An elegance, a splendor that belonged only to old aristocrats. Nowadays, even true aristocrats no longer exist. Everybody wants to be a businessman, a banker, make a lot of money, have affairs with actresses.)

I accelerate. Table 27 at Billares is usually lucky. I hope it's not full. Around nine at night, for four or five games, when I've connected with the lucky combination of numbers, I feel I can win.

Anxious, worked up, I reach Billares. The doorman, in his ridiculous green top hat, greets me: "Good evening, sir. Have you enjoyed your vacation? It's nice to see you again."

I would have to write an article about the bad taste of game rooms. This poor man, forced to wear that canary green uniform and that tall top hat. An article, in the weekly magazine with the highest circulation, has incalculable repercussions. (The tyranny of the majority that Steiner speaks of.) In the blinding light of the vestibule I wait for the green light to shine: ENTER. The most impatient drop coins in the slot machines that line the hall while the light changes (the red WAIT sign is lit).

Next to me, two women, loaded with gold bracelets and earrings, wearing masklike makeup, are waiting their turn to enter.

"He suffers terribly when I leave him alone," one says to the other. "I think he's a little depressed. The other day when I got home he had broken a flower pot. But I don't like to be his slave; I have to have my fun. The doctor says so."

In Las Vegas, these problems are resolved. In Las Vegas, the casinos have a free child care service to take care of children and domestic animals while the adults gamble. If you go to play the slots, bingo, or roulette in Las Vegas, you can leave your little cubs in the care of true professionals. It doesn't matter whether it's a dog, a cat, a cayman, or a penguin. Animals—whatever the species—need only two things: food and affection. Just like us.

22

'm a truly addicted man. I'm addicted to gambling, cigarettes, women, reading the newspaper, showering, life. I detest the certainty of being mortal. But others—those who don't gamble—also have their addictions. They're addicted to work, money, soccer, alcohol, medications, herbs, hipness, or style. There are religious addicts and political addicts. At least my addictions are lucid. And they don't harm anyone but myself.

(Lucia would say this is a self-justification.)

23

The small oasis of vacation has ended. Now everything starts all over again, monotonous, exactly the way it was: the search for exclusives for the magazine, the letters from the bank, the fleeting flirtations, the nights of gambling, the two weekly sessions with the psychoanalyst. Tuesdays and Fridays at the set hour, like old lovers. I visit her—she visits me—twice a week, separated by the office desk. I have still not made it to the couch, like the boyfriend who hasn't received the proof of her love. I know there are other men—and women—who are invited to recline on the sofa, but Lucia interviews me head-on, face to face.

On the first Friday after my vacation I tell her: "Maybe psychoanalysis is a game too, and I've become addicted to this game just as much as I have to the roulette wheel or the slot machine."

A game, with its set rules—twice a week, forty-five minutes a shot, the fixed price of each appointment, each game, the roles well defined: I play patient, she plays healer. In games, you can't switch roles. One is the bank, the other is the bettor. One loses, the other wins. But in chess and blackjack, you can tie: nobody wins, nobody loses.

"If you like that simile," Lucia accepts, "then you realize that there's something to win in our sessions, or games, as you like to call them. You've come to me to win something. So I help you win. Not to win at gambling, but at your own life. You're not throwing your money away for nothing in these sessions, the way you do with slot machines. It's investment, not squandering."

She sells her product well. She should be the managing director of a fashion magazine or a casino.

"The Japanese just invented a table game—a variation on Monopoly," I tell her, "where you buy women. The feminists have protested."

"Can't you buy men, too?" Lucia asks.

"No," I answer. "Homosexuality is not democratic, since it's in the minority."

"You seem to know everything about games," she says. I'm not sure if she's being sarcastic.

"One becomes a collector of that which one loves," I say. "You should know all about desire. Isn't that the subject of psychoanalysis?" I counterattack.

"One of the subjects," she says reluctantly.

"You've met one obsession, you've met them all."

"It *is* possible *not* to be obsessed," Lucia says.

I let out an impertinent laugh. "Then you would be patientless. Or with just one."

"You perhaps?" Lucia says quickly. "Is that your fantasy?"

Suddenly I realize that after me and my silly story, some-

106

body else comes in. Another man or woman. A psycho-analyst is like a mother with many children; no one is privileged. Each one wants to be the favorite; receive more love, more touches, more protection, more admiration. But she distributes her time and attention equitably; forty-five minutes for each one, same price. But deep down, each one believes he is the chosen one.

"That is a kind of love," I assure her.

"Yes," Lucia says. "The relationship of analysis is a form of love, but instead of an insane love, the kind you feel for gambling, it's a love that leads to freedom and internal independence."

"If it's love, there must be some pleasure," I suggest sibyllinely. "What is yours?" I ask spontaneously.

"I ask the questions, not you," Lucia protects herself, looking at her watch. "And it is precisely your pleasure, not mine, that concerns me—which we will discuss during the next session."

24

When ex-lovers don't want to see each other, it's because they're avoiding the feeling that their former passion was ridiculous.

Yesterday, the first day of my new life (I had solemnly promised myself not to gamble again after the ill-fated night I returned from *Chez Michelle*), I ran into Claudia unexpectedly on a street corner. Since our violent separation three years ago (reproaches and anger lack lucidity; they are ways of checking pain and depression), it's as though we lived on different planets. I might just as well have been living in a city beyond the Atlantic (there where my father disappeared), and she in some town in Normandy, like Madame Bovary. And between the two cities there is no mail, no message service, no telephone. We were also strangers before we met. The strongest passions are not experienced between similar people (protected by the sweet mirror of Narcissus), but between very different people. The differences become missiles, arrows, darts, canon balls, poison javelins aimed at an impossible target.

Drawn out from our respective worlds by the crazy explosion of passion, to love each other we had to agree on the language we would adopt (nothing is more illusory than a shared language), the meaning of the words, time, and space. To establish these exchanges and *harmonize* (like tuning a violin), we had only the ambiguous vehicle of our bodies. She had a mouth (with a slight nick on the upper lip that I loved, rendering her beauty more tangible), and I had a mouth. I had a pair of legs, and she had another . . . long, magnificent. Her belly was wide and accommodating, like the sea; mine, narrow. And we drank different things, we ate different food, we gesticulated with different gestures. But our cells, our tissue, the smell of our internal viscera, our ejaculations of sweat or semen, our humoral secrets, hurled us against each other, one on top of the other, one inside the other, in a desperate search for impossible unity.

"You are what you eat," Claudia said one day. (I had already heard that from Michelle.)

In that case, I am her (because she devoured me) and she is me (because I devoured her). And the separation was as violent as childbirth: visceral pain, blood, sweat, howls, expulsion, a broken umbilical cord, fear, loneliness, shock. "From that moment on," I told the psychoanalyst, "and for a long time after, I was half a man and she a 'broken' woman."

And yet, against all odds, yesterday, the first day of my new life, I ran into Claudia on a street corner. I thought it a ridiculous place to meet. Whenever desire, imagination, and anxiety—in those painful moments—made me fantasize about this scene, it always happened in her house, or

mine, under dim lights, with ample time; or I imagined it
to be in a hotel, in a strange place, where the weight of the
past was lighter. But fate had chosen a common, busy street
corner. I, who had renounced fate since the night before; I,
who believed I was a new man. I had renounced fate, but
fate had not renounced me. As we recognized each other, we
hesitated, like two awkward dolls. I stopped, indecisively,
and she stopped, insecurely. I felt like I had too many hands
(I didn't know what to do with them), and my legs weak-
ened and grew slack.

"Hi," I said, with the hoarse voice I save for emotional
moments.

"Hi," Claudia said, with less confidence than usual.

The change of the traffic light caught us off guard in the
middle of the street, and unwittingly we started to run
together. There was a café on the corner.

"You want to get something to drink?" I asked, without
too much emphasis.

"Why not?" Claudia answered.

I was annoyed. That was the kind of answer I hated about
Claudia; that simulated indifference, that way of hers of
dampening everything. In the end, all that remains of the
great passions are the repetitive obsessions, tics, a dark
anger from the failure and the certainty that none of that
can ever change.

She ordered a gin-fizz; I ordered a whiskey. That hadn't
changed either, the same drinks as always.

I lit a cigarette (so did she), and I looked at Claudia
dispassionately. Tall, broad-shouldered, pronounced cheekbones, thick lips, pale complexion, big, dark bags under her
eyes (as if she'd just come from an orgy). She'd lost none of
her strength, her attractiveness; yet I felt no desire. The

pain had sterilized it, eradicated it. She might have felt the same thing. We were two cautious ex-lovers who'd been burned by too strong a bolt of lightning, and now fearful, we avoided the shock.

"I assumed you were abroad," Claudia said.

People who call anything beyond the border "abroad" bug me. For example, to be in the next city is to be "abroad."

"Why?" I asked, concealing my irritation.

"You always said you didn't like the city much."

"I also said the opposite," I defended myself.

My interpretation was that upon breaking up, Claudia would have liked it if I'd left the city; a convenient way of erasing me, making me disappear. She moves from hunger to hatred with extraordinary ease.

"Are you still with the magazine?" she asks.

"Yes," I respond.

I was starting to feel like a criminal on trial. Claudia asked the questions, I answered them. That was the casting of the roles she liked. Claudia's biting, concrete way of talking had always bothered me. Nothing is harder to answer than direct questions; they preclude the possibility of doubt. And they're always about banalities. Well, to her, they're not banalities.

"And you, what are you doing?" I returned the question so as not to be constantly on the defensive.

She, however, doesn't like to be interrogated.

"The same as always," she answered.

How explicit! How sweet! How communicative! (I carefully guarded myself from expressing this praise.)

"So, you must be bored then," I ventured.

"I'm never bored," she declared, seething.

"I thought fickle people got bored," I said.

"How's it going with the psychoanalyst?" she suddenly asked.

I registered the blow immediately. How did she know I was in analysis? It was a trick question because naiveté in Claudia is unthinkable. If she was ever once naive, it must have been during her first seven days as an embryo.

"How do you know that?" I asked.

"I have my sources," Claudia said. "Or do you think you're the only one with information?"

I felt disarmed. I'm not inclined toward paranoia; we differ in that too. For a moment I thought cold Claudia might have been getting information on me through the new interns at the magazine or from my neighbors, or the waiters at the bar around the corner from my house. Later it struck me that that was what she wanted me to think. I decided to avoid that dangerous path.

"My psychoanalyst is very pretty," I said stupidly.

"I don't imagine you with a psychoanalyst who isn't pretty," she said. Fine, this was familiar territory. In reality, for the three years that our relationship lasted, when we weren't in bed, we were discussing the men and women that we'd each laid claim to. To Claudia (very masculine in this way), war is an active part of love and eroticism.

"We still haven't gone to bed," I said with a shamelessness that only one person in the world would believe: Claudia.

"No?" she said sarcastically. "How odd! Are you sick?"

We were bickering again, our usual way of relating to each other. Nothing had changed in some senses. Before, we bickered and then went to bed; or we went to bed and then bickered. A lot of adrenaline is released, estrogen and progesterone levels increase, but in the long run, it gets monotonous and uninspiring. At least for me. Now, we only lacked the bed.

"She doesn't want to," I said, almost complaining.

"You'll get her yet," Claudia said in an angry tone.

She stood up. I think she had obtained her secret objective: to leave each other again, annoyed. Annoyance was a good cure for nostalgia, pain, loss. Claudia never hesitated to employ subterfuge. She accepts her own frustration with dignity, as long as she gets the other's.

"We'll see you," she added.

Unfulfilled promises and deliberately debunked expectations floated in the air: the dull, gray residue of a dying conversation.

"We'll see you," I repeated to return the hope she wanted to frustrate me with.

When I was left alone in the middle of the street, I felt an unpleasant sensation of emptiness. I couldn't really remember what time it was. I looked at my watch. It was six o'clock. Time to go to the magazine. Had I eaten or hadn't I? The cold crepuscular light, milky and opaque, was like a spit in the face. The idea of going to the editorial office, hearing the phones, reading the faxes, choosing the photographs, was dreadful. Why didn't I say to Claudia: "I'm sorry. You don't know how sorry I am. You don't know how much I hurt. What a shame. I love you in some strange, detrimental but immensely compassionate way. I still love you." Then I smiled: what a delirious speech. Claudia doesn't go for such sentimentality. I never knew what the word meant. If I had managed to utter that sentence, she might have responded: "Not me. I'm quite fine the way I am." False. But some people can only sustain themselves by falsehood. Everything else scares them.

To make matters worse, now it was getting dark. What

was this coldness when everything was growing calm?

I looked from one side of the street to the other. Dark cars passed by. Street vendors selling paper napkins, pens, and candy took advantage of the red light to peddle their sorry products to hurried drivers—well adapted to the chaos of the world. Everyone plays his role. Some drive cars, others sell rolls of paper, pencils, or gum. I had to go to work. Detestable chronicles of society life: a party in Marbella, the Duke's divorce, the accident of the son of Europe's most handsome actor.

I hailed a cab. I sat back in the seat.

"To Billares," I told him.

I couldn't win. I just wanted to lose, the way I'd lost with Claudia. Unless Claudia was the one who had lost.

25

lost a lot of money last night," I confessed to the psychoanalyst during the next session. "I shouldn't have played. I had a foreboding, my favorite table was full, and I couldn't concentrate. But I got stubborn, and instead of quitting, I persisted. When I ran out of money, I left the casino and went to the nearest bank to withdraw more with my credit card. I was blinded. I lost more."

"How strange that so spontaneously you're talking to me about losing," Lucia comments. "Until now, you've never talked to me about money, as if you only bet plastic chips, dreams, desires, symbols. It didn't seem to bother you that you were betting money; money that you've worked hard for, seeing as you're not rich."

I never hid from her the fact that I have to work for a living.

"Talking about money bothers me," I say evasively.

"How curious that you don't want to talk about money," Lucia says, "in an era when most people talk about nothing else."

"It's noncommittal," I say. "What is the person talking about money really talking about. Not the money itself, not about an end, but about the means."

"Numbers are no less abstract, no matter how hard you try to fictionalize them and turn them into anecdotes," the psychoanalyst says. "Money and numbers have the same level of abstraction, no matter how much you love the legends surrounding numbers seven and nine."

The oldest croupier at the Monte Carlo casino—thirty years in the profession—maintains that seven and nine repeat themselves. He recalls one night when the seven came up nine times in a row, making a fortune for one gambler after he'd doubled his bets on that number.

"I can't afford both vices," I announce mean-spiritedly. "Gambling and analysis together are too expensive for me."

"Indeed," she recognizes. "You can't pay for both. But if you can scrape up the money to continue gambling, you can also get the money to come back here."

"You're a very expensive prostitute," I say. "I have never paid so much for a woman."

"I am not here as a woman," she responds, "but as a professional."

"Don't professionals have a sex?" I ask aggressively.

"Not while they are performing their profession."

"For having no sex," I say, "you have very beautiful breasts."

She ignores my observation.

"By alluding to me as a woman and not as a professional," she says, "you hoped you could cross the line. You hoped to play on a different field, to use terminology you find familiar. I'm not prepared to enter that territory. You and I have said nothing from man to woman or from woman to man yet. As the gambler that you are, you know perfectly well that one of the conditions of playing is to respect the rules, to play with the same cards."

I should have looked for an uglier psychoanalyst.

26

Social class also exists in gambling. For the poor, lottery tickets, football pools, bets of six out of forty-nine numbers (only fourteen-million-to-one chance). The crude, conceited middle class has the bingo parlors with their presumptuous decor and uniformed waiters serving coffee and French fries.

The upper class, always distinguished by the exclusivity of its entertainment, parades its tedium in the discreet and elegant Deauville casino (boasting an important impressionist tradition) or in Monte Carlo, the miniature kingdom of small scandals that generates long rivers of ink.

Many legal gambling places have private rooms where a select group with fat wallets and inexhaustible bank accounts play games of poker or blackjack. No one ever inquires into the source of this money that flows across the tables of these games like jets of black gold. Money is mysterious, much more so than sex, and confers respectability on whoever obtains or wins it.

I cannot play in that league. How much can some guy like me lose? His salary? Chicken feed to these heavyweights.

And he who has nothing to lose, has nothing to gain.

27

I n gambling houses, hidden among the players, there is always at least one plain clothes employee whose presence usually goes unnoticed. It is the physiognomist. Subtle, quiet, discreet, the physiognomist strolls between the tables, in inaudible shoes like someone looking for a place to play. In reality, the physiognomist takes mental pictures of the clients, recognizes the regulars, the occasionals, calculates how much they bet, how much they lose, places names with faces.

The physiognomist is a discreet, alert, objective functionary with no feelings. He's part private detective, part psychologist. He speaks to no one, smiles gently and aseptically, and accompanies the clients to the bathroom when needed or leads them to their seat when they've gone astray between the smoke and the crowd.

In general, the gamblers don't notice him, concentrated as they are on the game, on the white ball bouncing over the numbers or on the monotone drone of the numbers, like the saying of the rosary.

Previously, all physiognomists were men, but now, in many salons, there are women: unemployed graduates, girls new to the big city who share apartments with provincials; smart kids who no longer dream of marriage as their only function.

I bought Maria José a drink on the way out of the bingo parlor. She's the physiognomist of the place and so had already found out my name and knew I worked for a big magazine. Physiognomists can't reveal data on the clients to anyone but the management; they can't agree to interviews or make statements; they're prohibited from gambling in this or any other establishment, nor can they accept tips. I think she liked me. I wanted to write an article on this singular profession, and she consented, provided I not publish her name.

"I graduated in literature," she told me, "and this is the only job I could find."

Across from the bingo parlor there's a bar that stays open until dawn for the nocturnal gamblers who abandon the salon after losing and whose hangover from gambling and dissatisfaction delay their return home. The bar belongs to an émigré from Cadiz who has a great sense of humor. His name is B.B. Me. The wave of customers starts at three A.M., when the parlor closes. Constricted faces—bad mood or depression. There are two kinds of gamblers: those who swear they'll never gamble again and the next day forget their promise, and those who, after losing, anxiously await the moment they can return. I belong to both classes.

"We can speak to clients only outside the establishment," she tells me, "but not more than once, and it's supposed to be small talk."

"The hunter hunted," I say. "The physiognomist spies on gamblers in the casino, and is spied on in the street."

"Management contracts private investigators to follow our movements," Maria José says.

"Aren't you envious of the gamblers?" I ask. "No one stops them from playing, no one stops them from talking, no one controls them."

Maria José shrugs her shoulders. "They're controlled by the bank, the State, their spouse, significant other, or me. More than once I've warned a hardened loser lacking funds not to come back for a long time. Management doesn't want a gambler who commits suicide or robs or cheats to feed his addiction. It's terrible publicity. We prefer moderate gamblers or ones with solid economic resources. The loss of a client who's on the verge of depression or who robs his workplace so he can continue to play bingo doesn't make much difference. Those who gamble once a week or two or three times a month suit us better."

"All the same," I insist, "you're not entirely free. It seems to me you can only do what management wants you to do."

Maria José looked me squarely in the eyes and laughed.

"I am twenty-five years old, my dear," she answered quickly. "I have learned to accept the rules, and not to rebel futilely or dream too much."

"A veritable life manual," I say sarcastically.

"I detest romanticism," Maria José said. "I skipped it in school. And gambling is a romantic, I should say, sick hobby."

"I believe you're quoting Goethe," I observed.

"And you're quoting Dostoevsky," Maria José replied.

I like arguing with women; all discussion with the opposite sex is an erotic skirmish. There's not a lot of difference between wartime rituals and love rituals.

"How are physiognomists chosen?" I asked.

"There are admission tests. You have to demonstrate skills in observation, visual memory, deduction capabilities, and quickness of reflexes."

"Like driving a car."

"It would be awful to confuse one player for another," Maria José pointed out.

"Could you tell me, for example, the name of the woman seated next to me tonight and whether or not the guy with her was her husband?"

Maria José laughed. She had a pretty laugh, not shrill, a little mischievous.

"Is that why you bought me a drink?" She said, immediately suspicious.

"That's not the only reason."

"You're a nice guy, a loser, and your name is Jorge, a name I like," she said. "The woman who sat down at your table is Marta; she owns an antiques shop; she's your age more or less, and the man next to her was in fact her husband. An important real estate developer, well connected politically. They come once a week to pass the time. Whether they win or lose doesn't matter, but she seems to enjoy gambling."

That I had already noticed earlier.

They had arrived together at the casino. They surveyed the tables (like sailors on deck), almost all of them were full (there were a lot of people that night), and finally decided to sit in the two empty seats next to me. For a couple of rounds, I had been sensing luck prowling around me; it was my moment to win. That's why I was so annoyed by their interruption of the tenuous secret relationship with luck by choosing my table. He was over forty, blond and tall, with freckled white skin and watery, light, inexpressive eyes. A repugnant albino complexion, I thought. He wore designer clothes, Italian shoes, and had a French lighter, typical of these bourgeoisie; rich from speculation, the nouveaux riches. (My French grandmother, not my Spanish, had taught me very early on to distinguish original wealth from acquired wealth. The latter, the bourgeoisie, never manage to hide their lack of taste, its inherent pettiness, its ostentation.)

The rich real estate developer sat down at my table with a crisp, disciplined movement without greeting me. That was his technique: an icy indifference to paralyze the weak. She, on the other hand, Marta, as Maria José called her, was a charming, vivacious woman with brilliant, almond black eyes in a beautiful angular face. She had long, straight, chestnut-colored hair with gold streaks. Her expression was intelligent, firm, complacent. She seemed to have something hard to achieve: an appropriate self-esteem. The world is full of men with an inflated sense of self-worth and women with a lack of it. This has allowed them to relate to each other in the same way from the most remote times: through sadomasochism.

Marta greeted me pleasantly with a smile, while he, the indifferent glacier, ordered a whiskey, barely moving his lips. There are two ways to exercise power: with shrieks and sticks (the most common), and the other, more refined way, its opposite: silence and subtle contempt. He seemed expert in the latter.

I should have changed tables that night. But the appendage floating between my legs, that arrogant little dictator, ordered me to stay. It was attracted to that elegant woman smoking Marlboros between her long fingers, looking at me unmaliciously, nicely, exercising a complicity between addictive gamblers that she surely couldn't share with albino face. (This shark, this white whale does not tremble at the game table. Surely he plays hard in his office, with much more expensive pieces: land, buildings, bridges, tunnels, and railroad tracks.)

I didn't budge from the table, even though I knew that from that instant on, my luck (that had been approaching) had retreated. Luck is a demanding woman who requires the strictest, most severe loyalty. One distracted thought and she's gone. Luck no longer gave me priority. I had to compete for it with these two new rivals who'd appeared. Fine. If I was prepared to renounce the bingo game in favor of albino face, who was buying a "board" indifferently, the deal with Marta was still to be resolved. I liked her too. In the old days, in poker and dice, when there was nothing left to bet, you bet your wife or girlfriend. Farm, earrings, land, houses, and the woman. Times have changed, and albino face might have had a meaty checking account, but I was prepared to fight for his woman.

In the first game after their arrival, after ball forty-six, I was missing just one number: two. I noticed that albino face (who was a little further behind) looked at my board with a slight shade of envy. I was nervous and excited. I wanted to be triumphant before Marta, as males of the species are wont to do. I wanted to prove my superiority. Ball forty-seven: fifteen. Ball forty-eight: eighty. Ball forty-nine: twenty-two. Ball fifty: with number eighteen, a shitty old lady called "bingo."

The young white whale looked scornfully at my board, missing one number, and whispered: "Bum luck."

She, on the other hand, oblivious to this dark, masculine combat, said: "What a shame. I was sure you were going to win."

125

Okay. In Aix, when I was a child, the right of ownership of things was established simply by a look: "I saw it first" was the declaration for the title of ownership over the stone, the branch, the lost marble, the spider, or the girl with golden braids. He had seen her first, no doubt, and that established his ownership, but perhaps she—who was no stone or rusty key lost in a pasture—had something to say about it. And whatever she had to say, she wouldn't say in the bingo parlor but somewhere else.

Convinced of that, I stayed in the room betting a full round every time, even though my losses were already excessive. "If you want heaven, you have to pay," Michelle said from time to time.

On the fourth game, out of the corner of my eye I saw that Marta was writing a *yes* by one number and a *no* by another on the top board of the three she had bought. The odds of winning were good.

At ball forty-eight, she said in a soft, enthusiastic voice: "Twenty-seven. Come on, twenty-seven."

She looked at the two of us as she said it as if the nearness of luck would turn us into accomplices. We were the Holy Trinity and she the Virgin Mary, the Annunciator, the Bestower, the Plenum of Grace, the Welcome.

"Twenty-seven," the announcer's laconic voice sang out.

"Bingo," the he-goat yelled in her place. He had appropriated the winning board from Marta and raised his voice so he could be seen. She let him do it, not seeming to care.

28

Some regular bingo players—fiftyish, separated or divorced, with dubious jobs and professions—attempt to take the employees away from this work, as if they were prostitutes, and marry them.

"I'd rather grow old as a physiognomist than marry one of them," Maria José tells me at five in the morning at B.B. Me's. "They like to believe they have something to offer," she adds. "They're vain. They don't know that when one is offering, one is asking."

"Women are becoming too smart for men," I say.

Maria José sighs, then looks at me self-assuredly. "I always like guys who are in love with someone else," she says, and I take it as an allusion.

"And I like women who are in love with other men."

29

Where the ancients used to speak of vices, we moderns speak of addiction. Psychology has replaced morality. We call the vice-ridden *sick*. We call excessive pride *narcissism*; the desire for someone else's desire *envy*; jealousy we call *insecurity*; drunkenness we call *dipsomania*; cruelty we call *sadism*.

In Stockholm, the world's most civilized city, at every step you see signs that say: "Alcoholics are sick. We must treat them with affection." Fine. Likewise they could make a sign for gamblers: "Gamblers are sick. We must treat them with affection." We could add: "Be generous with them. Give them a raffle ticket, a lottery ticket, a combination for the horse races."

"Gamblers only count the times they win; when they lose, they hide it," Maria José says, as I drive her home at six in the morning.

"The best thing that can happen to a gambler is not to have anyone to tell that he's won, no one to tell that he's lost," I reply.

"They should tell both things," Maria José insists. She's a rationalist. (I could never go to bed with a rationalist; my cock grows sad with them.)

"No," I say. "No one talks about his failures. The papers don't publish them, they're not on TV, and no one has an affair because of them. Narcissism, like the phallus, rises with triumph. With failure comes a collapse of the ego, impotence, prostration."

"Bah," she says incredulously. "What does fate have to do with personal success? Whether your number comes up or not is pure chance, it has no merit."

This girl has not read Dostoevsky.

But I, who have read him, loathe his confessions, his pathetic entreaties to Anna, after losing, his attacks of remorse —only to obtain family alliances, earrings, and furniture —his epileptic fits—before or after gambling—as much as his euphoria when he won, his conviction that he had won because he was the best, the most intelligent. I'm familiar with that moment of glory; the moment when the prize falls to our number, or when the capricious ball stops on the black square we've covered with chips. I've won! I've beaten luck! Ergo, I am wise, I am God.

Yet Dostoevsky himself wrote: "Only in gambling and nothing other than gambling, does nothing depend on nothing."

All the power of probability, of science, technique, religion, psychology, the laws of physics—of all human dreams—comes tumbling down like a house of cards when confronted with the senselessness of gambling, the supreme freedom of gambling. "Nothing depends on nothing." Indifferent to merit, beauty, strength, genes, inheritance, hard work, morality, the numbers float in the immense bosom of irresponsibility, in chaos. Einstein, who believed in an intelligible cosmic order said: "God doesn't play dice with the universe." Now, as his theory, like all theories, slowly crumbles, God returns to the dice. So do I.

30

Don't tell me that now you've come up with some other erotic reason to return to bingo," the psychoanalyst commented the other day when I told her the episode of Marta and her husband.

I wonder if the psychoanalyst is jealous. She is a woman after all.

"Does it bother you that I'm attracted to another woman?" I ask insidiously.

"Would you like it if I were?" she stings me back.

"I would like it, yes," I confess defiantly.

I'm jealous too . . . of Lucia's other patients. I don't know how many or who they are. My visits to the analyst—like meetings of secret lovers—are surrounded by mystery and discretion, in this country where the unknown is scorned and rejected and where weakness and fragility provoke laughter.

"Do you have a lot of male patients?" I ask.

"Why are you concerned with the sex of my patients?" she interrogates. It's an old trick: answer a question with a question.

"Curiosity and jealousy," I confess. "I would like to know how many men I am sharing the same woman with."

"Are you worried about this because Marta is a married woman?"

"Before going to bed with a woman, I do not have the bad taste to inquire into her civil status," I say. "Like all rules, it has its exceptions."

"But you know she's married," the psychoanalyst insists.

"Are you married?" I counterattack.

"My civil status is irrelevant," Lucia escapes again. "You don't mind falling in love with a married woman but you fear she might."

"If you don't lose, you can't win," I say.

"Indeed," Lucia says. "If you don't lose, you can't win. To lose, you have your addiction to gambling; we still don't know what you want to win. You're too smart to believe you can win something outside yourself. It's something else, my friend, to want to pretend that you believe it."

I hate that protective, vaguely superior way she says "my friend." Every guy who goes to a woman psychoanalyst has to be a faggot. They're the only men able to accept the superiority of a woman.

"Are all your male patients homosexual?" I ask provocatively.

"Why does something like that occur to you?"

"A man who comes to pay for a woman's protection can only be an orphan or a homosexual."

"Orphanhood is a condition of being," she responds. "Sexuality, on the other hand, is a behavior. We are men and women, but sexual orientation is not determined by genital characteristics. Furthermore, you don't pay me to protect you and you know that. If you need protection, hire a bodyguard."

I think the mutual hostility we occasionally express during our sessions is a way of protecting our territory. She doesn't want me to invade hers with my erotic or intimate suggestions, and I get irritated when I can't lure her into a trick. The defense of our own territory in the face of attempts to invade make us maintain our mutual respect.

"If I weren't already a little sick of gambling," I finally confess, "I wouldn't have fixated on Marta. Gambling requires absolute concentration."

"A nice advance," Lucia confirms. "You've just told me that you felt a desire stronger than the one to gamble. We're well on the road," she concludes and opens the door for me to leave.

"We're well on the road," a compensatory, gratuitous sentence, while sending me off, perhaps to alleviate the agony of expelling me from her office, of abandoning me to my own obsessions, my fantasies. She throws me out, she banishes me from the warm office with the brown carpet and mahogany furniture; but, feeling a little guilty about it, she rewards me with an encouraging word. She opens the office door to put me back on the street, into the chaos, the battle, the game, the loneliness, and for that journey, she gives me her blessing. Like the priest in a school or a captain in the army: "We're well on the road, my boy."

31

The last sentence of Dostoevsky's *The Gambler* says: "Tomorrow, tomorrow everything will have ended." It is the futile hope of the hardened gambler who, after a disastrous night, promises himself to give up the vice.

Last night, after having played until three in the morning and having lost more money than I can allow myself (I'm very tolerant with myself), I went home obfuscated. Obfuscated: black, dark, like a wolf's mouth. I like this metaphor. An awful night. I didn't get a single line. What's more, Marta wasn't at Billares. I didn't concentrate on the game. I lifted my head over the boards to watch the big front door where I hoped to see Marta enter with or without her husband. Winners popped up around me, skipping over me, no doubt because I couldn't muster the necessary power of concentration to win. (One time Dostoevsky attributed a ruinous night in the Baden-Baden casino to the nervousness he got from a cigar-smoking gambler. Another time, it was a lady's irritating perfume. Furious, indignant, he told Anna, "I wasn't able to play well," because the perfume exasperated him.)

When Billares closed, I went back to my apartment, disillusioned, unsatisfied, sick of gambling. To make things worse, as I walked in, I tripped over the rug and twisted my ankle. What else? I'd forgotten to turn on the answering machine, and there was nothing to eat in the freezer. Nor did I have any sleeping pills. Okay. If I went back out I might be able to find a few dealers and drug addicts willing to sell me a little hash, but I didn't feel like going out. I felt obfuscated, nervous, depressed. I couldn't stop smoking and I wasn't tired. I played a game of electronic chess, superior level (my only consolation when I lose in casinos is to beat the machine at chess), but I lost again. One unfortunate move of the Queen's Bishop in a critical moment and my entire strategy hit the floor. (I'm too proud to replay the move with the retro button.)

My recent financial losses had me preoccupied, infuriated. I couldn't go on like this. I lay down, with the light off (at least I could save electricity), and suddenly in the darkness I started to imagine delirious plans to recover the lost money. I'll rob a bank. In modern, highly stratified societies, where people interact only with their equals: congressmen with congressmen (even those belonging to the opposition), military men with military men, lawyers with other lawyers, professors with professors, administrators with administrators, who would imagine that a reporter from the highest circulation magazine, with ten years' experience in the profession, as they solemnly say, would suddenly rob a bank? Bank robbers interact only with bank robbers. I am therefore beyond suspicion; as unlikely as a university professor, a doctor, or a lawyer. To each profession, its own crimes. A university professor can steal research from a student, a distracted doctor can leave a compress in his patient's belly, a journalist can manipulate, conceal, or sell information, but none of them can rob a bank. Of course, I'm not going to rob a bank the old-fashioned way, with a pistol and a kerchief over my face. I wouldn't know how; they'd catch me in a second.

Instead of robbing a bank the old way, I'll seize the cash from a twenty-four-hour teller machine. I'll access the vestibule with my credit card, and through an ingenious system, I'll remove the cash from the machine. But what is the ingenious system? I don't know anything about electronics. We all know about the excessive specialization of modern times. A journalist can't fix a plug and a stockbroker can't locate his mastoid. There has to be a way to deactivate the teller, confuse the machine's memory, and strip it. But that's too complicated for me, a literature major and reporter. A guy in love with words and with luck, but incapable of explaining electricity.

"Don't be stupid," I tell myself. "You don't have to prove that you're smarter than a cold, black bank machine. Once inside the vestibule, you take it by force and that's it." Force and abuse: two traditionally masculine recourses. That's how women, titles, land, and crowns were obtained and that's how wars have been won. You go in, approach the machine—fat like a pregnant woman—and you rape it, rip it open, gut it, smash it. OK, then. How much money does an automatic teller have? Will it be enough to cover my losses over the last few months? And what if somebody sees me? Suddenly it strikes me that surely there are TV cameras and alarms installed in bank vestibules. A tiny photoelectric cell concealed in the ceiling or in a doorjamb. I'll be photographed by a hidden, infallible eye, like the eye of God. Michelle told me that the first time I saw the image of the holy triangle with the eye of the All-powerful, I burst out crying. I was scared. It is an accusing, critical eye like the one in Poe's short story. Paranoid people, like Claudia, believe someone is constantly watching them; a persecuting look that passes through doors and walls, that has the power to read hidden thoughts, repressed desires. Nothing can turn that eye off, nothing can close it. The human look, by contrast, is desirous, born of greed. "I'll eat you with my eyes," is a sexual projection. *To see and want to see* is to want to take someone over. Fine. If God is in the bank vestibule, I'll have to find another way to recover the lost money. I detest specialization. I can interview an actress, analyze a poem by Baudelaire, write an editorial, and beat the chess video game, but I can't fix a TV, or lay bricks, or grow onions like Michelle, or rob a bank.

The other possibility is to counterfeit money. I feel a great sympathy for counterfeiters; by printing bills on their own, they mock the seeming seriousness of money. I'll counterfeit small bills, they're easier to introduce into the market. I can use them without much risk when I buy cigarettes, yogurt, or fish. I could also play bingo and roulette with the false money. That way, when I lose I won't really be losing. And if I win, I'll get good money. So long as they don't pay me with my own false bills. "Now you've discovered another way to continue gambling," the psychoanalyst would say.

I wake up with a hangover. Drinking's not the only thing that breeds hangovers; obsessive gambling does too. My tongue is pasty, I feel tired, my arms hurt, my movements are awkward and I almost slip in the shower. *Remorse*, that word I hate and Claudia was so fond of, is the best word to describe my condition. This morning I abhor gambling, even though just like drinkers, the morning malaise would cease with a new dose. Sometimes when I wake up saturated with gambling, after an obsessive night of betting, I go down to the corner bar and order a strong cup of coffee, and I start playing the slot machine. In some strange way, gambling again calms me down, makes me myself again. But today I make a decision: no gambling for one month. Not one lottery ticket. Not one coin in the slots. I'll ignore casinos, weekly raffles, the lottery. Just for one month. It's a truce, not an abandonment. Even the most hardened smokers (those who lose sight of themselves without the phallus between their fingers) are capable of quitting temporarily when they catch the flu or a cold.

The resolution to abstain from gambling for a period of time satisfies me for the moment. I'm a changed man. From now on, a new life. I'll whistle, I'll hum tunes, chew gum, drink juice, work out, and get massages. I'll go to the country on weekends. As for Marta, the elegant virgin of Billares, I can find her somewhere else, alone.

If I don't gamble, I won't go to analysis either. I'll kill two birds with one stone. And I'll save on both sides. I won't even say good-bye to Lucia. Analysis is a contract both parties can voluntarily break. She's not a lover; I can suspend our interviews without explanation. I won't go to tomorrow's session. I'll leave an excuse on her office answering machine. I'll tell her I'm going away for a month on business. That sounds good. Men without vices travel for business. The others, for pleasure.

"I'll sell you the Escort," I tell Santos, the magazine's photographer, that afternoon. He has always liked my white

Escort with the sunroof for "contemplating the stars," according to the salesman. He coveted the car at first, but couldn't bring himself to ask me to borrow it.

Like all insecure people, Santos is wary. He wanted it when it wasn't his, but now that he has the chance to get it, cheap, he can't decide.

"It's in perfect condition, man," I say. "I'm only selling it because I've lost too much money gambling."

He wouldn't do me a favor (for insecure people, doing favors increases insecurity), and even though the deal I'm offering is a good one for him, he also questions the advantages.

"Fine. If you don't want it, I'll sell it to the boss," I say. (The director makes a hobby of collecting cars.)

"Wait, wait," Santos says with the stinginess of insecure people. "Let me think about it."

"I can't wait. Look," I say, "I'll give it to you for three months, then you can sell it back to me at a higher price, Okay?"

"What if I don't want to sell it to you?" Santos says, wanting to play with all the advantages.

"If you don't want to sell it, I'll buy another," I say with infinite patience.

"You won't have the money to buy a new one," he says stingily.

"I can live without a car," I say. "I don't know if you remember, but Adam and Eve didn't have a car."

He laughs a little, the tension is eased. I ask a fair price, and in the end, still reluctant, he hands me a check. Suddenly, owning what he thought he wanted so badly doesn't make him happy, but only a little perplexed. I slap him on the back and say: "Emmanuelle, you know, the one who wanted to turn sex into philosophy, says true pleasure is desire."

The director comes into the office without a greeting, wearing an unfriendly expression. Not to greet: the privilege of people with power. For the cover of this issue, the model who's making it big in New York. Tall, long hair, tiny waist, pretty. She *doesn't* smoke, *doesn't* drink, *doesn't* fornicate, *doesn't* gamble—*light*. Ten thousand dead in El Salvador, assassinated by death squads. *Hard*—but El Salvador's a long way away: under ten thousand deaths and there's no story in the magazine.

"I have a slight fever," the director announces as he studies next week's media menu.

Nobel Prize winner in physics: seventy-three years old, gray hair, distinguished, doubts the existence of time. *Light*.

"Do kidney ailments make you feverish?" he asks me. He has more confidence in me as a doctor, which I'm not, than as a reporter, which I am, due to one of those strange hypochondriac fantasies. He's suspicious of his body but also suspicious of doctors.

"If you have an infection, yes," I say.

The Hampshire rapist: fifteen virgin white girls, meticulously torn apart, shredded, cut up, and buried. *Hard*.

"I think I lost a little blood when I urinated," he says.

I look at the calendar on the wall. "Then your period is early. Go see a gynecologist," I say.

He doesn't even smile. He calls his secretary and tells her to postpone all his meetings until tomorrow, he thinks he's sick.

The bullfighter's marriage with young socialite. Fifteen hundred guests, black-tie, honeymoon in the Bahamas. "We're very happy." *Light*. A transvestite beaten and

140

killed by strangers: members of an urban gang of vigilantes.

"*Hard*," I tell the director.

"*Light*," he says. "It was just a transvestite."

If they don't kill at least a dozen transvestites at once, there's no space in the magazine. We need it for the countess's son's new fling.

32

Threhe Antiques Gallery is on a main street. You enter by climbing a beautiful flight of wide, shiny jade-colored marble steps. The gallery is composed of a series of small shops with rugs that line the halls. It's easy to spend time in the leisurely contemplation of the exquisite objects on display: engraved marble thimbles, porcelain dolls in organdy dresses, pocket watches with faces of delicate Renaissance paintings, ebony distaffs, brass jugglers painted red, blue, and yellow, Chinese mah-jongg with their many carved pieces, and an English tea service with gold inscriptions on the bottom.

It's a quiet gallery, decorated with plants in enormous stone flowerpots, beneath a glass ceiling.

To each her own landscape. It seemed natural to find Marta there, mixed in among baroque secretaries, bronze angels, old paintings of shipwrecks bought in London, and modernist butterflies. For the discreet clientele looking at the display cases or flipping through the catalogs, the gallery pipes in soft classical music. Bach sonatas and Vivaldi concertos. The small extravagances of the bourgeoisie, I thought. Thanks to shady speculation, the great self-made businessman also acquires a pretty young wife, elegant, probably with a degree in Art History (Art is the Anti-History) and, along with the dishwasher, the house on the beach and the grand piano, gives her an exquisite antiques shop, crammed with objects that must be brought over from London, Flanders and Paris.

I found Marta's shop without much effort at the top of the stairs. Some antique shops specialize in toys, paintings, or crystal, but they all share that calm, mature atmosphere of collections undevoured by the cancer of hipness. In this one, there were some beautiful, oval daguerreotypes in lightly varnished wood frames and an odd series of turn-of-the-century miniature bathers posed quite gracefully over a base simulating a beach.

I went in and asked about the bathers. Since it was a little after midday, when stores usually close, Marta was alone.

"I'm your table companion, the one with no luck," I said by way of introduction as soon as she recognized me.

She laughed, and instead of the series of bathers, I saw the series of her perfectly aligned white teeth. Teeth are a sexual symbol, maybe that's why I fixate on them so much.

"Ah!" she said. "The reporter."

We were alone, not an odd thing at this hour in the Antiques Gallery.

"Are you a collector or are you writing an article on antique dealers?" she asked.

"I'm a collector with no money," I said, "and a journalist tired of his profession. Can I buy you a cup of coffee?" (The gallery has a pleasant cafeteria that's always open, where you can observe the various shop windows.)

"You can't," Marta said, "but I accept and, tell me, what do you collect?"

"Nautical things, like Neruda. But lamentably, I don't have a house on an island, nor am I an ambassador, I've never been married, and I don't write poems. I just have a few ships in bottles, the 'Ocean Queen' in an English coffee box and an embalmed mermaid I bought from a fisherman in the Costa Brava who thought she was real."

"You're either a liar or a strange man," she said as we sat down in the gallery's mirrored cafeteria.

"That sounds like a mediocre alternative," I said.

She laughed. Bernard Shaw said women are won by making them laugh—only slightly better than the old saying that the fastest way to a man's heart is through his stomach. But nobody reads Bernard Shaw anymore so that wisdom is lost.

"I can allow myself the luxury of fantasies," Marta said. "I don't work for a living, I work for pleasure. I adore objects. I have no interest in selling them. I like finding them, cataloging them, learning their history, and preserving them. When I sell one, I get depressed."

"You could keep them in your house," I say. "That way no one could threaten you by buying them."

"It wouldn't be the same," Marta says. "In the shop, I'm alone, it's my own space without foreign interference."

"A love affair."

"Possibly."

"A perverse love," I interpret. "You pretend you have a job when actually you have a house of call for yourself alone, full of objects of desire."

"You're going too quickly," Marta stopped me. We had ordered coffee. I love drinking coffee with women I want.

144

It's an act of complicity, like the cigarettes we light almost simultaneously. She Marlboro; I, Lucky.

"I studied art history," she tells me. "But I never imagined I could fall in love to such an extent. I have pursued one silver needle with an engraved bee from London to the Falkland Islands, from there to Mexico, from Mexico to Barcelona. It wasn't worth that much, but it was important for its itinerary, its biography."

"More than one man has done the same for a woman," I say.

She laughs again. "I wouldn't do it for any person, but for a rare piece I would."

"It's not the things we love that fill us with meaning," I point out, "but we who give meaning to the things we love. Besides, loving things isn't dangerous. There's no 'other.' Most of the time, you don't even need to know the name of the person who made the piece."

"I like *my* relationships with objects; that's my true vocation. I'm a fetishist, but not of just one object."

"Bravo!" I say. "I think you've found the way to avoid suffering."

"That is also a mediocre interpretation," she returns my observation.

"Could you tell me everything about the bathers?" I ask as an invitation.

She takes a sip of her coffee and smiles. "The bathers arouse everyone's curiosity. They must trigger some dark, collective fantasies."

With an unconscious gesture, she touches her wedding ring. She's dressed in black (a color that looks good on her); a fuzzy soft wool sweater, black skirt, and a modern mask of a woman where the neck ends. I have a thing about black, you can tell.

"I know you're married," I attack. "But desire is free and I want you," I say with complete sincerity. "We could talk about it over several afternoons, at this time, when the gallery's empty, mixing delicious stories of Chinese vases, glass butterflies, and bronze soldiers, or somewhere else, if you accept the invitation. Talking about desire kindles desire."

"I'm not sure you understood me," she responds. "I spend most of my time in this gallery. Disloyalty with objects is tolerated. I might be the only one who even knows it's disloyal."

"I know too."

"It's a way of life I find pleasing. I'm the owner of this museum as well as the restorer, the tenant and the guard."

"Something on the order of a vestal," I say.

"Maybe to you. To me, it's a way of harmony."

"And an evasion," I accuse.

"I feel no guilt," she answers quickly. "And I consider it gauche to speak of marriage or the relationships of our fellow men."

It's true. In order to desire, you have to forget reality. Desire is not inscribed within the order of reality, but rather the imagination.

"If you ever decide to break the crystal bubble, the glass museum," I say, "call me at this number. Fear doesn't protect us from anything. In fact, it increases fear."

"I'll cut myself if the glass bubble shatters into pieces," Marta says as she stands up.

"Psychologists say pain is a form of healing," I say as a good-bye.

While on my way down the steps, a tall, hefty man heading in the opposite direction bumps into me, knocks me off balance, and hits me in the stomach. Without an apology, he continues up. There are too many lunatics on the loose. When I reach the street, it occurs to me that the guy who tripped into me could be Marta's husband's bodyguard, and that the apparent accident was a warning. I immediately smile. Desire makes paranoid buds spring up in us. Desire makes us suspicious, fearful, dependent. We fear losing the expectation of pleasure that we've deposited in one person and we start seeing signs, traces of that suspected loss at every step.

At any rate, I feel content. Most men I know only like women for making love, even if they have to marry them. I, on the other hand, not only like to make love to them, I like to study them, watch them move, and, especially, talk to them. It's my feminine side.

33

At night, I take the last train home. Now that I've sold my Escort, I'm a pedestrian once again. The experience is not overly upsetting. The platforms at night with their neon lights and advertisements for American movies seem like a fallout shelter where pale ghosts, owing to the lack of oxygen, saunter like the last survivors of postindustrial civilization. There is no way to keep these tunnels, these cesspools of the world, clean.

It's eleven. The last trains take longer to come. They're picking up the stragglers, the vagabonds: that girl wearing a short yellow coat over black wool tights, with her spike haircut, smacking her chewing gum loudly in provocation; that lanky man with the torn jeans and greasy hair; that toothless old man mumbling to himself. The platform's lighted panel with the fluorescent red letters that move across the screen announces the public activities of the city for these last vagrants of the night, who ignore it. A symphony, an exhibition of paintings, an opera; then the weather forecast. The fall in temperature in the north, the beginning of a storm in the west, the wind speed and the tide levels. All this to find out whether or not you should take an umbrella tomorrow. Fine. The human being concerns himself only with the immediate. And the immediate, for the majority of any population, is whether or not it will be nice tomorrow. It's not an issue of choice but of instinct. In this regard, we're no different from dogs, flies, or elephants.

While I wait for the train on the illuminated, mostly empty platform, I think I am the last bachelor in the modern world. The *golden bachelor,* or something like that. I could star in a thriller with six hundred episodes before the happy ending, the wedding. Who would I marry? (If you're thinking Lucia, you're mistaken. Lucia's no good for the thriller since she's the psychoanalyst. The thriller predates psychoanalysis and women's liberation. Most men wouldn't know what to do with a psychoanalyst wife. And yet Lucia might be married. Had her husband been one of her patients? Did the therapy end in marriage? *To be continued.*)

A single guy goes home to his apartment on the last subway, opens the door, there's no one there, he roars with satisfaction, goes to the refrigerator, makes himself a sandwich with ham, cheese, lettuce, and tomato, opens a can of un-lite beer, looks out the window at the moving blue and red billboard for *El Gran Banco,* puts Tom Waits on the stereo (a record from his days as a drunk, single troubadour before he got married, which ruined his music), lights a cigarette, stretches his legs, and takes off his shoes. And if anything is missing to please him, he can put on a porn video and masturbate quietly, safely: there's no risk of disease and it's free.

Ah! He also listens to the answering machine to see if there are any messages.

"I should remind you that your therapy has not been terminated," Lucia's professional voice says in the machine. "I'd like to see you next week."

That I did not expect, though when I think about it, in consuming societies, it makes sense that the seller would do everything possible to keep his client. What's more, orthodoxy no longer exists anywhere and that is a wonderful thing. So, the roles have reversed: it's not me, the anxious patient, leaving a message on his psychoanalyst's machine, but her, calling me, searching for me, trying not to let me go. Does she need me or my money? (You're a stupid narcissist, like all narcissists. This call must be part of the therapy. If you feel solicited, like a lap dog, you will find the strength to continue. Orthodox interpretation.)

Before falling asleep, it occurs to me that my decision not to go back to her office is not exclusively due to lack of money. It's that I don't want to talk to the psychoanalyst about Marta. I want to keep this story to myself.

34

Three days later, at four in the afternoon, I show up at the Antiques Gallery. Marta is alone behind the window reading a book. I think how nice it must be to sit there among dark furniture, plush chairs, Victorian lamps, and antique toys. It's like a reading room. In urban apartments there's no space reserved for reading. There is room, however, for the TV, the spoiled brat of the house.

"I'm dying to know what book you're reading," I say by way of greeting.

She's surprised, pleasantly it seems (she hasn't had time to fake it). She closes the book as if it were an act of intimacy and says: "I am very private about my reading. I only mention it if I can't avoid it; reading is one of the few intimate acts of life and I don't want to defile it. But I'm pleased to see you again."

"I didn't come for you; I came for the bathers," I say,

teasing her, and I hand her the flowers I bought this morning: a small, mixed, wild-looking bouquet. "I wanted to see them again. They haven't been bought yet?"

"I'll tell you a secret," she says quickly. "I wouldn't sell them for the world. I like them too much. Sometimes I think they're my ancestors: old sisters I once had, playing innocently on the beach, oblivious to all onlookers."

She places the colorful flowers in a shiny black vase as if they belonged there between the sepia daguerreotypes and the theater binoculars.

"I knew you wouldn't call me and I wasn't prepared not to see you again," I confess. "No pressure. How about that cafeteria where nobody can see you?" I suggest.

Indeed, who could see us in the gallery cafe at this time, after noon, when the stores are closed and there are no customers?

"I'm a spoiled woman," Marta says when we sit down. "If I like something, I get attached very quickly. But I know it and sometimes I can avoid it."

"Why would you want to avoid it? Not all pleasure is harmful," I say and I get the unpleasant feeling that I'm trying to sell her something.

"I'd rather talk about the dancers," Marta interrupts.

"I don't like traditional roles," I say abruptly. "I'm not trying to be the seducer inducing you to do something you secretly desire or don't desire at all."

I think we're both uncomfortable, and not exactly because we dislike each other. My most intense relationships have been with women who made me uncomfortable and who I made uncomfortable. ("The only way to grow," the psychoanalyst would say, but she's not here, and all the better that she's not.)

"You're not going to tell me you believe in inducement,"

Marta says. "You can only advance that which already exists in some form inside."

I remain uncomfortable. She does too. I make one last effort to eliminate the verbal fencing at which we are both experts, since we're seducers.

"To be brief," I suddenly say, "what do you think about making love in my apartment at this improper hour, or do you know some other place or better time?"

The stab is deep and Marta spills some of her coffee on the table.

"Wait for me at your house," she says resolutely after hesitating for a moment. "At six-thirty. Does that work for you?"

I agree and go quickly. Leaving the gallery, no one trips me, but I suddenly realize it's closing day at the magazine and I'll have to walk over the director's dead body to get out of there by six. And since the director is a hypochondriac, hypochondriacs are the last to become dead bodies.

I enter the office like an inhale.

"What's wrong with you," the receptionist asks in surprise.

I don't answer and move on. That's how men of power act.

The director is already in the editorial room, yelling about some messed-up caption under a photo (a tennis player instead of an ex–government official who just died!). I bury my right arm inside my raincoat and go to my desk, moaning in a low voice. My desk is covered with paper and there are various phone messages written on my pad. Urgent.

I sprawl out in my chair visibly and I do nothing. The phone rings and I don't answer. It rings again. I know this infuriates the director on closing day.

Without raising his head, extremely annoyed, the director yells in my direction: "Pick up that phone or you're fired!"

I pick it up with my left hand. "It's for you," I say. "From Banco Central. The manager."

"I'm not in," he yells. "I'll call him back."

Then, finally, he lifts his head. He sees me laboriously maneuvering the phone with my left arm while I keep my right one buried in my beige coat.

"What's wrong with you?" he asks, suddenly interested.

"I'm not well," I say enigmatically. Nothing excites a hypochondriac more than an unnamed, unidentified ailment. All their fears, worries, projections spring forth, free and out of control.

"Well, what have you got?"

"I don't know. My elbow is killing me."

"Which elbow?" he asks, abandoning his absorbing task and approaching me.

"My right."

He is frightened when he looks at me. The worst is not what he imagines. He's much more afraid of what he definitely doesn't know, what he can't imagine.

"How long has it been hurting?" he says, alarmed.

"Since last night. I couldn't sleep it hurt so bad."

"What could it be?" he asks in a wisp of a voice. "You're never sick."

"Epicondilitis," I say abstractly.

He's been listening to me very attentively, now he holds his silence. I've got him with an ailment he's not familiar with and that makes him even more anxious.

"The so-called 'tennis elbow,' " I add.

He's perplexed. He's not familiar with the symptoms and fears he has epicondilitis and doesn't know it.

154

"But you don't play tennis," he notes. (He's saying it to himself; he doesn't play tennis either.)

"Tennis players aren't the only ones who get it," I inform him. "It's a muscular and bone inflammation that comes after an exertion, a bad movement or erosion from the friction of a tendon against a bone."

He adores pseudoscientific explanations. Others he finds impenetrable.

He reflects for a moment. "You got it from gambling!" he suddenly blurts. "You forced your arm while gambling!" he insists. He feels saved, free from harm, immune to the disease. He doesn't gamble.

"Maybe," I say. "It's killing me."

"And you still haven't been to the doctor?" he asks me.

"No," I admit. "Today is closing and I thought you'd need me."

"Don't be stupid," he yells. "I don't want sick people in the editorial office. Do you know how to treat 'that'? " he asks with disgust.

"I think with infiltrations and rest."

"Infiltrations? That must really hurt."

"There's no other solution. Otherwise, the operating room."

"Go to the doctor right now," the director screams. "Go to the hospital or whatever."

He identifies with sick people; he becomes paternalistic and tolerant.

I leave the magazine like an exhale. It's five thirty. In the taxi I pull my arm out of the raincoat and stretch it.

35

At quarter to seven, she's here. In the evening semi-darkness of this extended autumn (I've lit the softest lights in the room), her face gathers shadows that make it more profound, more intense: an addict's dark circles under her eyes. The kind I sometimes get from gambling, sometimes from working, sometimes from snorting and, less often, from making love.

We're sitting on the living room sofa facing the ebony table covered with a series of wooden and lacquer boxes that Michelle gave me when she decided to break up her collection. I added just one: the small metal box with sailor knots engraved on the lid.

She picks up that box delicately and caresses it. The movement gives me a quiver inside, and another one, very localized, outside. In profile, she places the box back on the table and I draw my face next to hers and bury my nose in her hair. It smells like wood, dry wood, like hashish. A strong smell that leaves a burning residue in my nose. She combs my hair with her fingers. Then she caresses the nape of my neck and I feel my nerves tense up like vibrating chords. I open the white silk of her blouse and the beautiful quadrature of her shoulders appears magnificently, then the arc of her shoulder blades (the only geometry I like), and the lace trim of her bra, just slightly paler than her blouse. No one can speak of these harmonies: when you actually find precisely what you were looking for, compared with what you imagined, it has a violent power of the real. This bedazzling can produce a frenetic nervous activity (the unbearable revolution of beauty) or a passive, hypnotized fascination. The former makes us awkward, confused, unsatisfied, as if we had to destroy beauty, annul it, in order to regain peace; the latter paralyzes us, transporting us to a contemplative, unnamed limbo. I attempted not to fall into the one or the other. I am a pervert according to traditional norms—or instinct—impelled to invade a woman as if she were a territory to be occupied, a fortress to besiege and storm; my secret pleasure is much slower, more minute and delicate: it consists of prolonging, surrounding, instead of attacking; exploring instead of invading, entertaining instead of violating. I have no interest in those uncontrollable explosions—like bursts of nature: primary earthquakes, devastating floods where, in the chaos of the destruction, everything mixes together, the organic with the inorganic, the horrible with the beautiful. Like painters who don't want to consider their painting finished and add a brushstroke here and one there, to me, love is a work where the most important thing is not the denouement, but how you get to it. And when you get there—because the inevitable destiny of everything is to conclude at some point—together with the blaze of the finale, I start to feel a kind of

157

melancholy: the kind when a work is finished. That which merits loving, should be loved unhurriedly, thoroughly. Only that which you want to abandon, to lose, should be done in agitation.

But one cannot dwell in beauty permanently. It is a refuge, not a home. I don't know how much time had gone by, nor how many times the work I don't like to finish had started and stopped, when Marta said: "I'm sorry. I am not a free woman. I should go."

Fine. She was a pragmatic woman.

She was getting dressed in front of the bedroom mirror so, lying in bed, I could see two Martas: the one putting on her blouse and silver earrings with delicate and elegant movements, and the other one, the one in the mirror, with the black skirt already pulled over her hips.

"Don't you have some kind of fixed quota of freedom?" I asked. "Something like every Sunday of the week or during summer vacation?"

She looked at me unannoyed. "I'd like to see you again but it won't be easy."

"I would be a jealous husband too," I admitted.

She laughed. "I can't imagine you as a husband."

"Thank you," I said.

Now she was going through her black purse as all practical women do. Everything in order after the amorous disorder: the keys, Kleenex, calendar, fountain pen, wallet, cigarettes, lighter, small appointment book, toothbrush, credit card, and the tiny Venetian pillbox, perhaps for her birth control pills.

I got dressed quickly. Pink shirt, beige pants, blue jacket. We both dressed like romantics, but deep down we were probably slightly classical: marriage, adultery, all that.

"I hate Madame Bovary," I said as we left the bedroom.

"Nobody would say that," she said smiling.

"Now I'd like to buy you a strong cup of coffee in a warm night cafe," I told her. "I really like talking after making love, in front of a couple of cups of coffee. But no one in this city has the coffee machine turned on after ten and you have to go."

She hesitated when she got to the door of my apartment.

"I have to go to London in ten days," she told me. "Business trip. I'm pursuing a porcelain doll made in Dusseldorf in 1939, signed on the neck. Apparently it's in the attic of an old, half-crazy collector on King's Road."

"Coincidentally," I replied, "I have to go to London in ten days. Business trip. I'm pursuing a romantic who believes she's a bourgeoise and reads classical poems in an antiques shop. I'm not interested in her owner. I've never believed in private property."

"That's why you're not rich," she said laughing.

I took her downstairs, stopped a taxi and we both tried to kiss each other good-bye discreetly.

I went back to my house whistling softly. It's a habit I've kept since childhood and practice only when I'm content, that is, when I'm in love with a gorgeous bourgeoise who I'm trying to turn into a romantic.

I opened the door off the street to my building. The vestibule was dark. I turned on the light. Then two enormous guys I'd never seen before jumped me.

They were kind enough to drag me, half undone, to my apartment door. They looked through my pockets for the keys, opened the door, and threw me in like a sack of potatoes, not without a warning, in case I was a little dumb: "This is just a warning, and if you persist, Don Juan, you won't be worth much." They gave me a kick in the head because they liked to finish things off good, and left me on the floor bleeding from the nose with a dislocated jaw and a broken arm.

When I could move a little, I got to the phone and dialed the director's number. He's the only person I know capable of getting up after one in the morning if a sick person is in need.

"What's wrong?" he asked me. "You sound horrible."

And he hadn't seen my face yet.

"I need a doctor," I mumbled. "Can you come by for me?"

"A doctor?" he repeated. "I'm getting dressed and leaving right away. Take an aspirin or something. And don't move. Sick people aren't supposed to move," he said and hung up.

Three days later, back in the editorial office, I got a short note from Marta. It said: "I've cancelled my trip to London. I hope you forgive me. Marta." On heavy green paper in a matching envelope that smelled of wood.

The anti-inflammatories were upsetting my stomach, which might have been why I wanted to vomit so badly. Besides, I didn't like the fact that it was autumn. It gets dark so early, you catch colds and everybody is depressed.

"I would really like to know what happened to you," the director had said, as the doctor was making the initial repairs. "I don't think it's from a gambling problem and you haven't been involved in any complicated investigations for the magazine."

"It's personal," I said curtly.

He looked at me with a certain respect. In his jargon, "personal" means "sexual," but it's a subject that inspires

160

mistrust and suspicion in him. He never thinks it's clean enough.

"Strange," he said. "You never get into this kind of trouble."

"I'd like to investigate the affairs of a certain successful and moneyed businessman, whose accounts must not be exactly clean," I told him.

He looked at me suspiciously. "No one ever has clean accounts."

"Simple, 'personal' curiosity," I added.

"Can you tell me who he is?"

I hesitated. I had planned to keep it a secret but now it didn't seem important. Besides, I was tired and depressed. The anti-inflammatories, no doubt.

"I know him," he said when I told him the name of the construction firm. "A small fish who's grown big," he added cryptically.

I was hoping to have won the director's complicity in spite of his being a volatile and easily impressionable man.

Despite my headache and upset stomach, I made several attempts, frenetic in fact, to obtain information about the dealings of the developer fish. Devoting myself to it made me slightly excited; it was all I could do and it seemed better than doing nothing. It brought me a kind of consolation. A new kid at the magazine, the kind trying to prove himself who takes orders without opening his mouth and doesn't ask questions, gave me the first facts. For the moment, he wasn't uncovering anything important: a few rigged contracts, a couple of concessions he obtained who knows how, and a public tender offer he shouldn't have won; nothing unique, nothing too scandalous.

My arm ached, plus the analgesics were rotting my stomach. Better go home. I don't remember going to bed before nine since childhood.

In one of his novels, Albert Cohen says Romeo never would have fallen in love with Juliet—and so no tragedy—if she had been old and toothless. Same with Calixto and Melibea. Therefore, the conclusion of the Genevan writer—love depends on things as subtle as the nasal appendix, the contour of breasts, the gesture of holding a cigarette between one's fingers, or of moving one's hips. "Stupid," I say, now in bed, to that other appendage located below my abdomen, to whose stimulations I am so sensitive. But the woman Cohen loved most, Jane Fillion, the inspiration for *The Master's Beauty*, was not the fairest of them all. If he loved her so intensely, it was because intelligent, sensual, passionate Jane loved women. Definitively not being able to possess her, Cohen assured the perpetuation of his desire. Passionately loving women, Jane was the *missing* thing that propitiated the writer's desire. As if she were someone else's wife.

They separated after two years of a tortuous, violent, hostile, and dazzling love. From the debris came *The Master's Beauty*. (One loves better in memory. The poets learned that in the beginning of the beginning, if ever there was a beginning.) Some people make pyrotechnics from debris. "You don't even do that," I say to my lower appendage that doesn't dare make itself too manifest from the thrashing. "Coward," I add. "I could write the saddest verses tonight," my member mumbles listlessly. "Somebody else has already written them," I answer.

One time I asked Claudia if she spoke to her sex and she answered me no, and that she didn't know a single woman who did. Here we have a fundamental difference. At some point in his life, if not every day, a man, heterosexual or gay,

162

talks to his sex. There are some who draw him a face, eyes, and a mustache. It's a way of laughing at him, of taking away his transcendence. I'm too proud for that. I like his autonomy, even though it harms me. But if I had to do something with him, instead of painting two eyes and a mouth, I'd transform him into a missile in the shape of a penis, baptize it with an affectionate name, as they do their cocks, and launch it against the enemy, who in turn possesses several missiles of the same size, in the shape of a dick nicknamed with funny diminutives. And the war of missiles, of cocks is established.

The phone rings. It's the boss. He asks me how I feel. I tell him I'm playing war.

"You're doing well," he says. "Watch TV, play chess, rest, and take the anti-inflammatories."

"I'm playing the war of dicks," I say. "A missile, a dick, a dick, a missile. Let's see who wins."

There's a silence on the end of the line.

"Don't you have a mother somewhere?" the boss suddenly remembers. "Why don't you call her and tell her to come take care of you? I think you're feverish."

"War is not a woman's thing," I say. "It's a virile invention. Of men, only for men."

"And the psychoanalyst? Why don't you call the psychoanalyst?" he insists.

"She's a psychoanalyst, not a babysitter," I say and hang up.

36

The promising young reporter waits for me at the magazine with various papers in his hand, proud of himself (ever since my arm's been in a sling, I get to the office earlier). He's discovered a crooked deal of significance in the investigation I asked him to do. Well, well, Marta's husband, through false corporations that existed only on paper, monopolized all the Public Works concessions of a government official during the year 1986. Later, as he saw fit, he distributed them among companies of friends who paid him big money for the orders. The affair has never been uncovered and could have political connections.

Here we have how someone who doesn't even have a missile can have a bomb, I say to myself. I'm going to ask the director to put this kid on the payroll. He deserves it.

With the papers in hand, I enter the boss's office. He's in

front of his desk screaming into the phone. We've lost an exclusive. What exclusive? The bullfighter's wedding or something like that. What happened? Did the competition offer more? Nobody really knows what happened. I don't either. He hangs up, infuriated. He looks at me with a none-too-friendly face.

"I got it!" I exclaim euphorically. (Depression-excitation, stages of the manic-obsessive.) "I have documentation of the developer's racket. Several thousand million. All that's missing is to find out who's protecting him."

The director looks at the papers I give him. I wait calmly. I can't understand how this affair hasn't blown up before. But now I'll turn him into *polvo*, dust. Where did the *polvo* metaphor come from? Surely some guy, after an intense session (why do I think the session was with Marta?) felt tired, destroyed and said *"Estoy hecho polvo,"* and it stuck. Given this new meaning of the word *polvo*, the biblical phrase has an interesting rereading: "Ashes to ashes, dust, *polvo*, to dust."

After leaving through the pages attentively, the boss says, "interesting, but impossible."

Ashes to ashes, dust to dust.

"What are you saying?" I ask, surprised.

"I said: 'interesting, but impossible.' "

This is the way he is with the magazine: decisive and cutting.

"Why?" I'm overwhelmed.

"I too have verified something," the boss adds. "A lot of those millions stopped in the same place they came from," he insinuates.

"The government official?" I ask.

"Exactly, my dear," he says. "A little circulation of

money, the wheel of fortune or whatever you want to call it. He who gives, receives, or any other title you want to give it."

"All the better," I say. "I'll make the government department topple too. Two birds with one stone."

The director looks at me with a kind of paternalistic benevolence. I know, even though I never had the opportunity for my father to look at me this way.

"You go to bed and take care of that inflammation in your eyes," he says. "I don't know if you know this, but the government office finances a lot of our advertising, and furthermore, I don't want them closing down the magazine on me."

"We have more advertisers than we need," I answer.

"From this moment on," the director says, "consider this whole affair a 'confidential matter.' There was no investigation, nobody knows anything, and you got hit by a car. Fortunately, nothing serious. But you need rest. Take two weeks' vacation."

He immediately calls the kid I asked to do the research. "Where are you keeping this information?" he asks him in a neutral, inoffensive voice.

"In my computer, sir," the kid says naively.

"We're going to delete it right now," he says and he gets up to verify the operation. "Jorge's going to take two weeks' vacation to recuperate. For the next two weeks, you'll take care of his workload."

I leave the office furious. I want to meet Marta somewhere, even if it's right in front of the idiotic building developer, that self-made man under the protection of a government department. I head for Billares. With a little luck (it's eight at night), they'll show up, a bored and mediocre couple burning off their tedium while the neutral voice of an employee reels off the numbers of the balls. Balls. Maria José told me they usually come once a week. I hope today is that tiresome day of the week.

The Billares doorman (the penguin dressed in green) greets me less festively than other times. He's noticed my swollen face, my arm in a sling. "Everything okay, sir?" he says discreetly.

"Everything's fine," I answer.

I sit down at table twelve, not one of my normal tables, but it's close to the entrance. From there, I can easily discern the players already seated and those who appear when the green light in the hall goes on, like the starter's gun.

The round table twelve is occupied by a fat, ruddy, fortyish woman with the look of a middle-class single girl, that is, covered with gold trinkets, bracelets, and exaggerated makeup who's left the fox terrier yelping on the terrace. The unsatisfied women of Chekhov's stories walked the little dog along the bridge or by the train station at dusk as the long gray and pink clouds stretched out like their sighs. A century later, unsatisfied women come to the bingo parlor, take a chair at the round table, place their cigarettes, lighter, and thick pencil next to the boards, and listen impassively to the chant of the balls. They could either get bingo or an older single bachelor inclined toward marriage.

The board seller drops off a board, recognizes me and murmurs: "I haven't seen you around here in days."

I smile at her a little. In the end, it really is like a brothel. "Good evening, sir, how are you? Can I offer you a small orgasm? Or do you want a big orgasm? The girls will be with you in a moment."

They are not in the room. They haven't arrived yet if

167

today is their night of entertainment. The twerp must be attending to his numerous affairs over the phone and Marta, after closing shop, would have gone to change her clothes.

I'm not concentrating on the chant of the numbers, and the rounds go by without my changing tables or seats. The fat woman next to me is getting into a bad mood.

"They're not calling anything on this side," she mutters.

I have no desire to talk and I don't respond. This is the first time I'm hoping for a different kind of prize.

Suddenly the access door opens and in the midst of the smoky room and the combination of lights (chandeliers, TV screens, reflections from the vestibule), I see a couple appear with an idiot leading the way; my heart jumps, but I've got the wrong fish. It must be a sturgeon or a conger eel and I want that idiot sea bream for dinner tonight.

"A round, sir?" the new board seller says. There's been a change of shifts. I don't know this girl. At the pace of one board per game, I'll be broke before Marta and her husband arrive. All the better if Marta comes to play alone this time.

By twelve o'clock, I start to believe they're not coming. I'm a man of long hopes and firm convictions: stubborn. It's taken me four hours (twenty-five rounds) to convince myself that I won't see them tonight. I haven't won a thing, not even a line; I'm not concentrating on the game and besides, my head hurts. The fat girl left some time ago. She got two lines, recouped some of her money and, convinced that this was not her lucky night, she left. Now sitting next to me is a curious couple, a tall blond foreigner and a swarthy Philippine woman fondling each other and playing one board between the two of them. She, in love and content, happily jots down the numbers and almost won the last hand. I have the feeling she'll win. That moment of absolute glory that

168

happens once in a lifetime: the man of her life, found by fortune, and a lucky board coinciding.

If they haven't come by twelve, they're not coming. The habits of marriage are overwhelmingly monotonous. Marta must know that well. For all these days (since the beating) she hasn't tried to call or come near me. Just that brief card definitively suspending our date in London. Fine. If she considers the affair over, why don't I do the same? Just one more episode of life in the meaningless melodrama written by a drunk writer (bad Shakespearian paraphrase). I should be able to get up from the table, leave the room, and go home. Take a tranquilizer, sleep. But it's hard to accept a final period placed by someone else. The final period is something one likes to insert oneself, like the phallus or the ball.

I don't see Maria José anywhere. But I do think I see another physiognomist in the room: a guy of medium build with an anodyne look, strolling along silently, filing through the tables with the grace of a dancer. But he scrutinizes the bettors like a distant father. The one I didn't have. The one who didn't watch me.

At one thirty, I step out for a minute, leaving my cigarettes and lighter on the table, to withdraw cash from the nearest machine. I feel like I'm on a slope, sliding downward in a vertigo that's both pleasant and unpleasant at the same time. Someone should stop me. But why? Life is a toboggan: an old metaphor from Tangier.

I go back to the room, convinced I won't find Marta and her idiot speculator tonight, nor will I win. It's not even about winning anymore, but about recouping some of my losses. But I won't win because I have no affectionate relationship with money. For me, money is a river (transitory, fluid), not a house to inhabit.

At three in the morning, only we obstinate losers are left in the place. Very few of us, all alike: skinny guys dressed in black, with bags under our eyes; smokers, loners. Brothel or bingo parlor, what difference does it make? The few women in the room are not alone and they are not true gamblers: bored, they're just keeping their stubborn husbands company. If it were up to them, they would have already gone to bed.

In the penultimate game I call a line, innocent and naive, not worth anything, but at least it's of a feminine nature.

"Bad luck," says the man sitting at my table. "It could have been bingo."

Killjoy.

I take a taxi back to my apartment. The lit-up city is deserted and the lights hang from the trees like wreaths at a party. It's the city's moment of beauty: alone, cold, static, like a painting hung on a museum wall.

"There's not much work," the cab driver says. "I think I'll go home and go to sleep."

I have the crazy hope that when I get home and listen to the answering machine, Marta's voice will emerge with a message. I wonder which is the last thing we forget about people who've died: their image or their voice. With my great-aunt in Aix who helped to raise me, years after she died, the first thing to go was my most recent images of her. When I had only one very old image left, I realized I'd lost her voice too.

I enter my apartment building with caution. I'm not completely sure that another killer hired by the idiot speculator isn't hiding behind some column or under the stairs to finish the job.

I turn on the lights in my apartment, go to the stereo, put on *Greensleeves,* a smooth, traditional melody written by Henry VIII and rewritten by more than a hundred composers. I walk over to the answering machine. I rewind. I hear Lucia's message: "I'm reminding you that you should set up your next visit tomorrow morning." Well, a discreet way of not accepting my abandonment, a confused tactic of denial. Or is it that I owe her money? I can't really remember if I paid her for the last session or not.

Abandonment: I don't want to accept Marta's abandonment, and the psychoanalyst doesn't want to accept mine.

"Abandonments are very painful," the psychoanalyst said once, referring to the absence of my father. I'm sure it hurt Michelle more than it hurt me.

37

ast night was the last night. The decision had been forming itself inside me, obscurely and unconsciously the way an embryo, a fetus, a new creature gestates. In the morning (a fair, almost wintry morning when everything is sharply visible, as if the cold were a diamond cutting the edges), I woke up with the conviction that that had been the last night.

I went down to the corner bar for breakfast like I do every morning. Coffee and a croissant. The bar owner greeted me. "How's it going? How's the magazine?" he said as he warmed my cup.

"I don't know," I said. "I'm on vacation."

He looked at my arm in the sling and seemed to understand. Like almost everyone who thinks he's understood, he probably didn't understand.

Then I went to the magazine. In a taxi.

Without knocking, I went into the director's office. He

172

was on the phone. When he hung up, he looked at me and said, "What are you doing here? I gave you fifteen days of rest to calm down."

"I'm calm," I said. "And I'm telling you calmly that if there's no denunciation, there's no returning."

It's possible that he'd forgotten the subject or already relegated it to the attic of the past. When he realized what I'd said, he fidgeted in his chair, raised his arms and screamed: "Are you crazy? Do you realize what you're saying? Or did that kick in the head completely do you in?"

"If there's no denunciation, there's no returning."

"An employee can't place conditions on me, you idiot."

"I know that from a certain point of view I can't nor is that what I intend," I said, "but from another, I must."

"This is ridiculous," he sputtered. "You know perfectly well there are a dozen people who want your job, or mine, or anybody else's. We're in a competitive society. No one's indispensable; the only thing indispensable is money. I can replace you in a second. Who do you think you are?"

"I know I'm not indispensable and that you can replace me in a second. I also know there are people who would like to see that happen. But you'll have to make the decision."

"What will you do? Grow potatoes? Row a wooden raft across the Pacific? Become a monk? I don't think you've won the lottery," the boss said.

"No," I said. "If luck's involved, I always lose."

"Ah!" he said. "I get it. You've got to win somewhere else."

I was not expecting a sudden fit of intelligence on his part: frivolous journalism had dulled him.

"Where and what I should win is my business," I said. "And it's not about winning but about feeling pushed too far."

"Idealism died with the seventies," the boss said.

"But malaise did not."

"Take some aspirin, start working out, buy yourself some Italian ties, or get an Arab lover."

"I'm already familiar with that prescription," I said. I got up and added, "When you've made a decision, let me know."

Perhaps I was going to lose this round, but at least luck wouldn't be the deciding factor. The end was going to be decided between the boss and me.

At five that afternoon, when the doors open, I went into Billares. The room was lively. It was the beginning of the month, the bettors had money. I chose a table with its back to the access door and decided to break the evil spell of this place where I always lose.

I played dispassionately and unfrenzied. It was my farewell. I wanted to finish quickly and get out of there.

Two hours after I'd come in, I called special bingo. It was the first time I'd ever called a special; that hardly ever happens.

I took the money with no emotion. I didn't leave a tip. I didn't care about breaking the rules. I bet again. On the hour, I called bingo again. I then took all the money I'd won and stuffed it in my pocket. I paid my table's drink tab, bought a complete round for the two remaining gamblers, and left.

At eight that night, I had an appointment with the psychoanalyst. It had been a while since we'd seen each other, since my resolution to quit gambling and before I'd gone to bed with Marta. I couldn't remember if I owed her a session, but I did remember her insistence that I continue the visits.

She was in front of me with her little book of notes on the

table, the green banker's lamp turned on, and a cigarette butt in the silver ashtray. The fine delicate Waterman like a paperweight was on top of the papers, a phallus in repose. She made no comment, despite seeing my arm in a sling. Whoever talks exposes herself, leaves her flank open. Those are the rules of the game, I didn't make them up. If I were to refuse to talk, she wouldn't talk either and, given that I am supposed to talk and she to interpret, the session would elapse uncomfortably into silence.

"Last night I quit gambling definitively," I announce unemotionally. "I'm probably out of work as well. And I got beat up for sleeping with Marta, a married woman, a woman with an owner, that is. I got beat up for having transgressed the law," I conclude.

"A lot of things in a short time," Lucia observes.

"I didn't want to lose Marta," I say. "But even she might not be able to win herself. I don't care about the job, and as far as gambling is concerned, I believe I want to prove to myself that I can quit. There's only one thing left for me to quit," I add and I pause.

Unknowingly, she has grabbed the Waterman.

"What?" she says in a neutral voice.

"You," I answer.

"If you're referring to analysis" (the precision is subtle: Do I want to abandon her or analysis?), "that decision seems premature. The work we've started together is not over."

"I came to see you of my own volition," I remind her. "I leave by my own volition, too."

"I'd like you to tell me how you reached that decision."

I interpret that as a delay tactic. Surely, if I describe that process, she'll find a fissure from which to prolong the sessions.

"Listen," I say, "I could have not come to say good-bye;

I could have abandoned this process without visiting you one last time. But, like all gamblers, I'm very fond of forms and rituals."

Now she's made a note on her notepad. I can guess what it says: "Like all gamblers, I'm very fond of forms and rituals." Will she publish an essay?

"Let me remind you," she warns, "that this is not a game."

"Sometimes," I say, "only one of the two is playing. I believe that psychology manuals call this a perversion. We could say that *your* perversion is observing, studying from the other side (from the office) someone else's perversion. A risk-free form of pleasure."

"If you're interested in the relationship that grows between a psychoanalyst and his or her patient, write a book about it. For the moment, that is not our concern."

"I would need the notes," I say.

She did not expect this attack. My mention of her notes has been a surprise.

"I would like to have the notes," I say. "In the end, I have paid quite a lot of money for you to take them."

"As a gambler," she says, "you're perfectly aware that your request is not within the rules of the game. It is inadmissible."

"I've come to inform you that I'm quitting gambling, and analysis, if they're not one and the same thing," I say.

"If they are the same to you, you know perfectly well that in gambling, someone loses and someone wins. What do you think you've won?"

"There are other options. There are ties, and there's also abandoning the game."

"Neither of those can be very stimulating to a gambler," Lucia says.

176

"I've become a humble man," I joke.

Now, though she's not taking any notes, she brandishes the Waterman between her fingers.

"I think that just as Marta has 'left' you," Lucia interprets, "you would like to 'leave' me. You avenge the abandonment of one woman with the abandonment of another."

"No," I correct. "I would love to invite you for coffee, and then to a hotel. I've been trying to tell you that all this time, but you haven't wanted to admit it or accept it."

"In that case," Lucia says, "you would avenge the abandonment of one woman by sleeping with another."

"But not with just any woman," I accept. "You."

"The more significant, the better. Your narcissism wins," Lucia says.

"I thought your duty as a good psychoanalyst—man or woman—was to reestablish the wounded narcissism of your patients."

"But the way to go about that," she admits, "is the choice of the professional."

"My narcissism has improved immeasurably," I admit. "Ever since I freely opted to quit gambling, and I prefer to think that I did not do that for a woman but for myself."

"That's the most sensible thing you've said so far," Lucia smiles.

"If you call me 'sensible,' I just may run right out of here and go straight to a casino. Like Don Quixote," I add, "sensibleness kills me."

"I thought your subconscious 'other' was Dostoevsky," she points out. "He quit gambling too, according to what you've told me."

It seems we've imperceptibly begun another session.

"There's a slight difference," I explain. "Dostoevsky quit gambling and went on to journalism. He was named the

177

director of Moscow's most important newspaper. But he didn't just run it. In reality, he wrote it almost entirely himself. The political articles, the social chronicles, the art criticism. A task so absorbing, he couldn't do anything else, for all that time. The only thing he didn't do was set up a stand under a street light and sell it."

"Which has no relation to your magazine's kind of journalism," she observes with apparent objectivity.

"Times have changed," I admit.

"Yes," Lucia agrees. "If you wanted to say something, you would have to write a book."

I wonder if she's suggesting something.

"Don't be absurd," I say. "Writing is senseless. You don't make a dime, it's exhausting, it awakens the envy of others, and its end is uncertain."

"How curious. That sounds like a description of gambling." She consults the notes and reads my description out loud: "You don't make a dime, it's exhausting, it awakens the envy of others, and its end is uncertain."

"If it were a description of gambling," I correct her, "it would be missing one element: pleasure."

"Maybe that's also what's missing from your description of writing," she says. "Doesn't that strike you as the only possible justification of an act that doesn't earn you a dime, is exhausting, awakens the envy of others, and whose end is uncertain?"

"It must be very pleasant if it costs so dearly," I venture.

"Don't tell me it hasn't occurred to you before," Lucia reproaches me, inadvertantly targeting me with her Waterman at the ready.

"Stop aiming that erect phallus at me," I yell, sick of watching it.

"It's a pen, just a pen," Lucia apologizes and lays it back

down on the table, in a neutral zone, equidistant from both of us.

"I think that if you have asked for my notes—which, of course, I will not give you—it's because you've fantasized about and wanted to write a book, but you're afraid to admit it. In case you fail, in case this time you don't manage to realize your desire, you have decided to suspend the sessions. If you lose, you don't want witnesses to your defeat. You yourself once told me that the casino gambler who bets against luck, not against human beings, is a person who can't stand to feel watched when he's losing. He gambles alone, wins or loses alone. No one can share the loneliness of writing either."

"I have decided to take charge," I say, without correcting her assumptions, "of my fantasies and desires, alone."

"That is a mature decision," Lucia accepts. "But sometimes it's advisable to share the load."

"If that is an offer," I insinuate, "I'd like you to repeat it somewhere else, outside the office."

"That's to be seen," Lucia says. "For the moment, we are trying to find out whether you have in fact managed to develop a desire other than gambling, and whether that desire is to write."

"My father wanted to write, at least according to Michelle," I resist. "But who could verify that? True desires are unutterable."

"That's why you still haven't said you want to write," Lucia concludes. "And now, let's respect that silence in which the desire is gestating, growing, like a new creature."

Unwittingly, I have grabbed the Waterman that was between us. I play with it between my fingers, like a woman's breasts. Like a penis.

"I'm not sure," I say dubiously. "I haven't said anything."

"Indeed, you have not said anything about that desire; you have not promised anything."

I fiddle with the Waterman between my fingers.

"I'd like to have access to the notes," I request again.

"No," Lucia says severely. "One thing is one thing and another, another. My notes are my work. I take them and I am responsible for them. You wouldn't submit your manuscripts to just anyone who asked either."

"That's true," I admit.

"As for the sessions," Lucia proposes, "we can take a break. Two, three weeks, a month, however long feels right to you. Then we will see each other again to continue the process."

"However, I might not want to see you inside these four walls, but somewhere else," I hint.

"It might be," Lucia admits. "And I might or might not accept."

I stand up to say good-bye. This time, given that the next session is a long way off, I extend my hand. She responds in kind. But then she looks at the office desk and says: "For now, the Waterman is mine. I believe you've inadvertently grabbed it."

I laugh. In fact, I had put it in my pants pocket.

"I think I should buy one," I say and I give it back to her.

The last sentence of *The Gambler* is: "Tomorrow, tomorrow everything will be over."

On the way back to my apartment, after the session, sunk down in the backseat of the taxi, I write on the white lip of my cigarette box: "Last night, last night I quit gambling." It seems like a good beginning.

180